To Susan —

A friend of long-standing
(some of it standing behind
a dull table!)

Best Wishes

Bev V.

NEITHER RAIN NOR SNOW

Beverly Vertrees

MINERVA PRESS
LONDON
MIAMI DELHI SYDNEY

NEITHER RAIN NOR SNOW
Copyright   Beverly Vertrees 2000

All Rights Reserved

ISBN 0 75411 189 X

First Published 2000 by
MINERVA PRESS
315–317 Regent Street
London W1R 7YB

Printed in Great Britain for Minerva Press

NEITHER RAIN NOR SNOW

Neither rain nor snow nor heat nor gloom of night stays these couriers from the swift completion of their appointed rounds.

William Mitchell Kendall
McKim, Mead and White
Architects of New York Post Office

Dedicated to my three: Carol, Sue and Bill,
with grateful thanks for their support and assistance.

A Joy to the World?

'Peace on Earth, good will to men.'

The sounds of carols played on loudspeakers came from the small radio shop halfway up Main Street. The streets were crowded with last minute shoppers; laughter rang out, friend greeted friend, clerks were harried, tempers flared and husbands moved through the mêlée with glazed looks, frantically searching for a suitable gift, because tomorrow was Christmas Day. Falling snow made the scene unreal – a Currier and Ives print in modern setting. But one jarring note went unnoticed by the scurrying shoppers, something never included in the placid, respectable lithographs of Mister Currier and Mister Ives. In the darkness at the end of Main Street, a portly, expensively-dressed man lay face down in the snow, and small dots of red spotted the clean snow on the post office steps. Christmas red. Blood red.

Captain Charles paced the floor in his office, asking the ceiling why in God's name these things happened to him.

'Christmas Eve!' he exploded. 'And one of those screwy ones.'

Sergeant Perolli nodded gloomily.

'Why do these things happen to me?' Charles repeated for the fifth or sixth time. 'Tell me, Perolli, how does a man get himself murdered – and he *was* murdered – a man can't stab himself in the back, walk all the way down the steps, get rid of the weapon, and then collapse! But how in the…'

He broke off and jerked open his office door. 'Did you find her yet?' he yelled.

The murmur on the other side of the door must have satisfied him, as he resumed his pacing, but Perolli decided he had slowed down a bit. Charles pounded one fist into the palm of the other hand and continued, 'How? Perolli, how in the world did he get himself killed on Main Street on Christmas Eve with no footprints around him, except for his, going down the steps? This is worse than one of those foolish "locked door" mysteries the fiction writers like.

'You would think, with all the shoppers milling around tonight…'

A discreet knock on the door interrupted his tirade and he barked, 'Come!'

The door opened and a patrolman stuck his head around the door frame.

'Mrs. Edwards is here, Captain,' he said.

'Good. Good. Send her in,' Charles answered, rubbing his hands together and backing up to lean one hip against his desk.

'Yessir,' the patrolman answered, withdrawing his head.

A moment later, a woman in her early fifties entered the room. She was a small woman, with silver gray hair, made slightly blue with a rinse. Her figure, obviously well cared for, was that of a much younger woman, short and of slight build. Her upright carriage showed a certain arrogance, as well as a rigid exercise program, or, as she was obviously well-to-do, perhaps her own personal masseuse. She wore a navy blue wool dress that fell midway to her ankles, a mink jacket and small mink-trimmed hat. Feet that looked to be about a size five were encased in fur-trimmed, brown leather high-heeled boots. She was perfectly at ease, though more than a little annoyed at being asked to come to police headquarters, and impatient to be on her way.

The patrolman who ushered her in pulled a chair over in front of Charles's desk and with a nod in his direction, she sat, folded her hands in her lap and looked inquiringly at Captain Charles.

'You wanted to see me, Lieutenant?' she said.

'Captain, Mrs…'

'Captain, then. You wished to speak to me?'

'Yes, Mrs. Edwards…' Captain Charles suddenly felt ill-at-ease, as though their positions had been reversed and he was the one being interviewed. He pulled himself up from the edge of his desk, cleared his throat and replied, 'We asked you to come here, because we have some unpleasant news, and we also have a coupla questions to ask you.'

'Unpleasant news, Lieutenant?'

'Captain, Ma'am,' Charles muttered.

Mrs. Edwards showed her annoyance and said, 'What unpleasant news and what questions could you possibly have for me? Come now. Get on with it. I have appointments to keep.'

'Well, Ma'am, it's about your husband,' the Captain began.

Mrs. Edwards sat straight at the edge of the chair, feet together rigidly. She snapped, 'Jerome and I have been separated for five years, and nothing he would do could possibly concern me in the least.' The ice in her voice was evident.

'This isn't something Mr. Edwards did, Ma'am,' Charles said. 'It was done to him. I mean – well, you see – uh, well, Mr. Edwards was found about an hour ago. He's dead, Mrs. Edwards.'

Captain Charles peered closely at the woman seated in front of him as she absorbed his news.

'God, she's a cool one. Hasn't turned a hair,' Charles thought.

In chilly tones, Mrs. Edwards said, 'Is that your unpleasant news, Captain? It is more like a very welcome Christmas present. If that is all, I will be going.'

She rose and gathered her fur jacket around her shoulders. Captain Charles realized his mouth was open and closed it with a snap.

'No! That isn't all! Sit down!'

'Really, Lieutenant, umm, Captain,' she sniffed.

'Please,' Charles added, more calmly. 'Sorry, Mrs. Edwards. Your reply just startled me. Look, there's more. Your husband didn't just up and die. He was murdered.'

Captain Charles waited, but when there was no further response, only an icy stare, he continued, 'We know that you and Mr. Edwards have been legally separated for some time, but we thought you had the right to hear about this from us, and we also thought you might be able to help us in this matter. Do you know of any reason why he would have been at the post office tonight some time after it had closed?'

'No, I do not.'

'Do you know of anyone who might want to kill Mr. Edwards?'

His visitor looked scornful. 'The population of this town is about nine thousand,' she said, her head held high. 'I would say there are approximately 8,999 people who might have a desire to see him dead.'

Charles again held his mouth open in amazement, then looked appealingly at Sergeant Perolli. Turning back to the woman in his office, he said in a tight voice, 'Mrs. Edwards, is there any help at all you can give us towards finding his murderer?'

'None whatever, Captain,' Mrs. Edwards answered coolly, 'except to wish you no success in your investigation.'

This time, Mrs. Edwards stood and swept out of the office before Charles could recover his voice, and closed the door quietly.

Charles walked around the desk and fell into his chair, wiping his forehead with a large, wrinkled handkerchief.

'Lord!' he gasped, 'Cool as a cucumber! Didn't turn a hair! Just like an ice maiden!'

Sergeant Perolli winced at the continued flow of clichés, but nodded agreement to his superior's comments. Charles slumped in his chair and restlessly drummed his fingers on the desk. He was a big man, and his uniform stretched tightly across his shoulders. Gray, crinkly hair circled a large area of pink skin, making him look like a well fed monk and his permanently red face became redder still as he thought of the interview terminated so quickly. His manner, like that of a large elephant trying to tiptoe through the jungle, made people think he was blundering and inept, but convicted criminals knew to their sorrow that an agile brain lay below the gray halo.

He had been in law enforcement work in the city for several years as part of the police department there, then had returned to his home town of Sunbury six years prior to this, to become its Chief of Police. He was happy to be back among long-term friends and glad to be rid of the pressures of big-city crime fighting and the frustration of city politics it involved. Happy, too, to be working closely with his boyhood friend, Anthony Perolli.

Perolli was a perfect foil for Charles's bombastic nature: a calm, reserved man of middle age, always extremely neat in his dress and retiring of manner. Standing about five feet eleven, with compact stature and military-like bearing, he kept himself in good physical shape by exercising regularly at the local health club. He was a confirmed bachelor. Charles and his wife had tried in the past introducing him to single women they thought likely candidates for marriage, but they had given up years ago when it became obvious that this was the life he preferred. The law was his wife, his child. He had worked in this police department most of his adult life, joining the department after a stint in the Air Force and then a two-year course in law enforcement at the nearby community college.

He and Captain Charles were contemporaries. Both were native Sunburyans, had been through grade school and high school together and worked well as a team.

Charles roused himself now and turned to his friend and colleague.

'Perolli,' he said, 'Go get me all the stuff they've dug up so far, will you?'

The sergeant pulled himself to his feet and left the office. In a few minutes he was back with a thin sheaf of notes which he placed on Charles's desk. After reading rapidly through the notes, Charles groaned and tossed the papers aside.

'Just like I said, Perolli,' he sighed. 'A screwy one. Here's Edwards at the bottom of the post office steps, dead for two hours or so when we brought him in, the ME says. And his watch was broken, probably when he fell, stopped at 5:30. Well, so far it makes a little sense. It's dark there by the post office, actually darker than usual because that street light is out. And since it's at the end of Main Street and closed at five o'clock, nobody would be going by there. So, he wasn't found until Amos Miller happened to go over to put some letters in the mail box. But what's impossible is the fact that he must have been stabbed at the top of the stairs. The post office doors were locked. He couldn't have been in the building, yet his footprints and the blood stains begin at the top of the steps, and nobody else's footprints are there. The snow began just after five. I was sure of that and the weather people confirmed it. 5:07 they said. That would be after the post office closed, so the snow was fresh and clean, just those footprints that match Jerome's boots. There was no blood or anything else inside the building, even supposing he could have gotten through the locked door. Now, by all that's holy, how did he get up there without making footprints going up? From the looks of it, he flew to the top of the steps, stabbed himself in the back, then staggered down to the steps to collapse at the bottom. Ah, Perolli, I should have taken up chicken farming.'

The Captain looked wistfully at the snowy scene outside his window. Snow was still falling and the weather forecasters predicted another two inches before morning, when it was supposed to stop. A nice Christmas Day, with the traditional white landscape that so delighted children and their nostalgic parents, but not that with which these policemen enjoyed contending.

Charles sighed again and glanced once more through the reports Perolli had handed him.

'But, you know, what's almost as bad,' he continued, 'is that we don't have a firm motive yet, just a whole mess of suspects. If the motive was just plain hate, we can suspect most everyone in town, and a few neighboring towns to boot! Mrs. Edwards was sure right about that. Jerome Edwards made enemies like Mr. Ford makes motor cars. He turned them out like an assembly line, a dozen at a time! But, just for the few who were, shall we say, close to our Mr. Edwards, they all have good reason for wanting him dead. His wife now…'

Charles ran a finger along his collar, thinking of the cool disinterest his news had met.

'His wife,' he went on, 'hated the man for pretty good reasons, and she surely wasn't shocked when we told her what had happened. I don't know what I expected – shock, surprise, glee? But not this – this nothing! I didn't expect her to swoon at the news, or jump up and down and dance around the room. But this icy calm – not a flicker of an eyelid. Do you suppose she already knew? Either because she knows who did it, or maybe because she did it herself? They say a knife is a woman's weapon, don't they? Wouldn't put it past her. She's certainly a cool, contained lady. For one thing, Jerome Edwards ruined their daughter's marriage when he was campaigning for District Attorney. That makes her daughter and son-in-law good suspects, too. His business partner was ruined when Jerome pulled a fast one and took over the newspaper. Several people got smeared in that dirty campaign he ran recently. That was a couple of months ago, but I'd say the wounds are still fresh.

'Then there's his brother-in-law, Johnny Stevens. Remember the scandal Jerome stirred up? Accusing John of stealing from the United Way Funds. Johnny was proved innocent, but there's a lot of bad blood there. The list goes on and on. Edwards didn't really have any friends – real friends. Oh, sure, he was into a lot of things, committees, organizations and the like, and he pulled a lot of weight in the state. I'm sure we'll find a lot more people who couldn't stand the man as we get further into this investigation. He seemed to enjoy stirring things up and making the fur fly. Stepped on a lot of people in the course of the year and before. He had "influential" friends in state politics but I wouldn't call any of them real friends. Any friends he might have had he alienated along the way.

'For that matter, we might as well include ourselves in the list. Edwards was trying to shake up the police department with all those editorials he wrote for his paper. And if he had been successful, you and I could have been out looking for other jobs.'

Charles glanced sideways at the sergeant.

'You didn't kill him, did you, Perolli?'

Sergeant Perolli shook his head, with a grin, and went back to inspecting the toes of his regulation shoes.

'Well,' Charles said, as he pushed himself upright. 'Guess there's nothing for it but to go talk to some of these people. Come on, Perolli. Grab a pencil and let's go celebrate Christmas Eve.'

Hark! The Herald

December 24, P.M.

The police car proceeded with some difficulty up the snowy, slippery road leading to the Point. Snow plows had been out this way, and snow was piled at the sides of the road, giving the driving a feeling of moving through a tunnel. And more snow had fallen since the plows had done their work, so that Perolli drove slowly and carefully, mindful of the dangers as he maneuvered the car around curves and steadily climbed the hill. The scene was beautiful, trees loaded with fairy dust-like powder, moonlight picking out branches like arms covered in silvery jackets. The purr of the car engine was the only sound to be heard as there were no other cars on the road but this one, and judicious residents were keeping to their homes.

The only habitation in this lonely section of town was the big, old, sprawling house that had belonged to Al Wagner, and was now, and had been in all the years since his death, maintained by his wife, Ethel. Ethel Wagner, known as Aunt Ethel to much of Sunbury, was Jerome Edwards's aunt. Nearing eighty, she was a descendant of the original settlers of Sunbury. Born in the town, and apparently intending to die there, she seemed to know everyone in the town and held open house up here on the hill.

Built in the eighteenth century, the house they were approaching was a mixture of architectural types. The original house was of white clapboard, two storeys high, with several dormers jutting from the roof. Wings had been added in more recent times, housing more bedrooms on one side, and kitchens, pantries and storerooms on the other. Ever since it was built it had been known as 'The Elms', though no elm trees now remained on the acreage. But the name stuck, and very few people in the area were unaware of the house and its present mistress. The Elms was a local landmark and Mrs. Wagner a local celebrity.

No call for help ever went unanswered by her. All of Sunbury knew what a soft touch she was, but no one ever took advantage of her generosity. From the lowliest to the social elite of Sunbury, 'Aunt Ethel' was loved and respected by all.

As they neared the house, the policemen saw lights from the windows sparkling on the snow. A lighted Christmas tree showed in a wide window, and a large wreath adorned the front door. A low fence at the entrance to the driveway was decorated with tiny white lights and greenery, and more lights festooned the low bushes flanking the front door.

Perolli parked the car close to the entrance to the house, and they walked up the two wide steps and rang the doorbell.

As she heard the door chime, Ethel came to answer its summons. A sweet-faced woman, with a pouter-pigeon shape and snow-white hair, she moved quickly across the polished floor of the hallway. In spite of her wealth, much of it inherited from her business tycoon father, she employed few servants. A cook-cum-housekeeper was not only an employee, but a cherished companion. A groundsman and a maid responsible for most of the cleaning completed her roster of servants, though others were brought in from time to time for heavy cleaning and when there were guests.

She opened the door and said, 'Why, good evening, Captain Charles,' as a blast of frigid air blew into the hallway. 'What brings you out here in this weather?' She pulled her cardigan more closely around hunched shoulders.

'Evening, Ma'am. I have some serious news and I'd like to come in and discuss it with you,' Charles replied.

'Well, come in. Come in and get out of this cold. Do knock the snow from your boots, please. Good evening to you, too, Sergeant Perolli.'

Perolli smiled and nodded, took off his cap and followed the Captain and Ethel into the house. Ethel led them to a small, bright and cheerful room, furnished with chintz-covered sofas and well polished maple furniture. There was a blazing fire in the stone fireplace, its light reflecting in the picture window opposite. Candles burned in many holders around the room, from wall sconces, and silver candlesticks on end tables as well as a group of seven or eight candles of differing heights on a table in the corner shed a warm glow.

Perolli chose a chair near the door, shoving his gloves into his pocket and tucking his feet under the chair, avoiding a multi-colored braided rug, and doing his best not to drip melted snow on the parquet floor.

'Please sit here, Captain,' Mrs. Wagner said, indicating a low chair at right angles to the fireplace. 'Get yourself warm. It really is cold out there tonight. It must be something very important to bring you all the way out here, on a terrible night like this, and on Christmas Eve, too.'

She sat across from him on a small sofa.

Charles carefully lowered his bulk into the chair and began, 'Mrs. Wagner, there has been...'

At that moment they became aware of raised voices in another part of the house and Lydia Ramsey came running into the room.

'Aunt Ethel! Father's dead, and we have to warn them...'

She broke off suddenly when she saw the policeman sitting by the fire. She was obviously upset, and her long brown hair, pulled back and fastened at the nape of her neck with a large tortoiseshell barrette, was coming loose and tendrils of hair hung across her brow. Lydia was a young woman of twenty-five years, with a long-legged, trim figure. At the moment she was short of breath from her precipitant rush into the room, and her cheeks were red from cold and excitement. She stood irresolute halfway into the room, both hands to her mouth. Charles struggled out of the low chair, and stood.

'Hello, Mrs. Ramsey. Who is it you think should be warned?' he asked.

Lydia, in confusion, stammered, 'Why, no... no one, that is, I meant tell... Oh, Aunt Ethel, this is so terrible!'

She ran to Ethel, who put her arms around her great-niece, her eyes wide as she gazed over Lydia's shoulder at Captain Charles.

'Is this the news you came to bring me?' she asked.

'Yes, that's it. Will you both sit down and listen to me? Maybe together we can make some sense of this.'

Ethel kept hold of Lydia's hand and pulled her down next to

her on the sofa. Holding tight to her hand, she said calmly, 'All right, Captain. Tell us about it. Was it an accident? Heart attack? What happened?'

As the police captain told the women the facts as far as he knew them, they sat very still, listening to every word, Lydia's hand captured tightly in Ethel's lap. Charles told of finding Jerome's body at the bottom of the post office steps only a few hours before this. He told them it was definitely murder, not an accident, and that so far, they had no idea who might have killed him, or how it was done. When he told them about his interview with Lydia's mother, they both started and spoke at the same time.

'But why bring Mother...'

'Marjorie would have nothing...'

Charles waited as they looked at each other and quieted.

'She hated your father, and with good reason, I might say,' he said to Lydia.

'She's been separated from him for five years,' Ethel protested. 'They would have been divorced if her religion allowed it. Surely she had more reason to kill him many years ago than now. And I certainly can't see Marjorie doing anything so violent. It's just not in her nature.'

'Many killings are done by those closest to the victim,' said Charles. 'And that is usually the first place we look. We had to talk to her. And besides, she certainly had a right to know about this and to hear it from us. Do either of you know of anything that has happened recently that would have altered that relationship?'

Both ladies shook their heads negatively.

'Nothing your mother has said, or anything you might have heard or seen?'

'No, Captain. I'm sure Mother hasn't seen or spoken to my father in a long time.'

'Okay,' Charles said, then, looking around the room, he asked Lydia, 'By the way, how did you get here? I didn't hear a car and you didn't come in the way we did.'

'I came in the back way. There's a trail through the woods that we always take. It's a short cut.'

'But not too well plowed I would imagine.'

'No, but I had the jeep and it can go about anywhere.'

Lydia was close to tears as she stood suddenly and cried, 'I must go to Mother now. Aunt Ethel, will you be all right?'

'Of course, child. Run along, and give my best to your mother. Judge Laurence will be here shortly to take me to the Christmas Eve services, and we'll see you all here tomorrow. Now do be careful going back down the road.'

She kissed Lydia's cheek and gave a small push to send her on her way. Lydia hurried from the room toward the back of the house, with a backward look at the policemen. They listened as they heard her retreating footsteps, then Charles stood and said, 'I'm sorry to have to bring this news to you, especially on Christmas Eve, but I wanted to tell you about it before you heard it on the news or somewhere. Sorry about the way it came out.'

Ethel turned back to Charles saying, 'The post office, you say. How very odd.'

After a moment she said, 'I know Jerome had made a lot of enemies in the past, but somehow *murder* never entered my mind. Are you quite sure, Captain?'

'Yes, I'm afraid so. It couldn't be anything else.'

Gathering his hat and gloves, Charles said, 'We'll be going along now. If you think of anything that might help us solve this thing, will you call us?'

'Of course, Captain. I'll do whatever I can. This is a terrible thing.'

'Maybe you will hear something that will help us. I know people talk to you, and tell you lots of things. You're a good listener.' Charles smiled at Ethel and patted her hand. 'Just think of all I've told you.'

Ethel smiled at him and turned to Perolli as he stood in the doorway.

'Please, you be careful too, driving down the hill, Sergeant. It's quite treacherous. I probably should stay home myself tonight, but I do hate to miss the Christmas Eve candlelight service.'

Perolli tipped his hat and followed Charles out the door and down the walk to the police car. At the car Charles said, 'Let's go take one more look at the post office. Maybe we missed something the first time. Drop me there, then go roust out Harold

Duane and tell him to meet us there. We'll need his key.'

They drove slowly down the winding road.

The Postmaster, Harold Duane, was indignant at being asked to leave his home on Christmas Eve, and stammered and sputtered like fat in a frying pan when he arrived, out of breath and angry, at the post office, joining Charles and Perolli. Charles had been walking up and down in front of the building.

'This is outrageous! I finished a busy Christmas season and finally got to go home and rest, and now you've dragged me back here again! Your superiors will hear about this!'

Harold was a short, skinny man, in his early forties, with receding sandy-colored hair and a prominent Adam's apple. Bundled into a red plaid jacket and hunter's cap with ear flaps down, and unbuckled old-fashioned galoshes, he gave the appearance of the town idler, rather than a man of some importance in a responsible position in the community. A long black scarf, wound around his neck and covering his jaw, completed his attire. His bulging eyes snapped and his mouth was a thin line.

'Easy, Harold. Easy. We didn't ask to be out working on Christmas Eve either,' Charles said. 'All we need is to have you let us in the post office. You heard about Jerome Edwards's murder?'

'Yes, yes, of course I heard. That kind of news travels fast in a town like this. And my assistant called me when he was asked to open the building for you. Wasn't that enough? Why are you insisting that I open up again for you?'

'This is your responsibility, I should think, Harold. And we just wanted to take another look. See if we missed anything the first time. And just maybe you can point out something that would give a hint of a clue to this killing. After all, this is a major crime, and Edwards was an important member of the community. We need to solve this as fast as possible.'

'I guess so,' Harold sullenly replied.

'And his death is going to be big news,' Charles added.

'You're right about that,' Duane answered. 'And now he can't have me removed as Postmaster. He was certainly trying.'

'Now, that would be a good motive for murder, wouldn't it?' Charles said, his head on one side as he grinned at the man.

Harold paled and gasped loudly, sputtering even more.

'No! No, I didn't mean... well, he was... oh, I didn't kill him! Much as I disliked him, and much as I'm glad he's dead. Anyway, I've been at home ever since I left the post office this afternoon. Ask my wife! Ask my son!'

'We will, Harold. We will. Now, will you open the doors for us? It's getting mighty cold out here.'

'But he was found outside the building. Why do you need to go inside?'

'He had to come from somewhere. He didn't just land at the foot of the steps. And the obvious answer is that he was in the post office building. Come on, Harold. I'm freezing my toes off.'

The three men had been stomping their feet and swinging their arms, trying to keep warm. Duane was shaking so badly, not only from the cold, but from anger and nerves, that it took several stabs at the keyhole before he could get the first door open, then the second door into the post office. Entering the building, Perolli and Charles gazed around the lobby, looking for any clues that would help solve this mystery. Many footprints crossed and crisscrossed the lobby floor, evidence of a large number of customers on this last day before Christmas.

The temperature was only a little better than the outside. The post office would be closed tomorrow, so the thermostats had been turned down, ostensibly saving the taxpayers' money, but the trio could see their breath as they talked together.

'Do you realize there were people actually mailing Christmas cards today? Why don't they listen? We keep telling them – mail early! But do they pay any attention?' Harold groused.

'Sure, Harold,' Charles said, his mind on the appearance of the lobby.

'Do you see anything here that is out of order? Anything that shouldn't be here, or anything at all unusual?'

Harold peered around the area. 'No, and I hope the cleaning crew will come in soon. Such a mess! Just look at that muddy puddle of water over there!'

Charles turned to look in the direction Harold was pointing. He frowned at a good sized puddle, apparently melting snow from someone's boots, in the corner of the room, before a narrow door. It was far away from the normal traffic pattern of the lobby.

'Where does that door lead?' asked Charles.

'What door? Oh, that. I really don't know,' replied Harold. 'I'm not sure it's even a door to anywhere, it could just be made to look like one to balance the door on the other side of the front doors. And that one's just a closet. If anything, this door could lead to another closet, too. But we never used the other one, so no one ever bothered with that door. I have no idea why they were ever built like that.'

Charles pulled his attention from the corner of the room and glanced around. The dirty footprints seemed to follow a regular pattern, back and forth to the counter, to the post office boxes and the mail slots.

'Could someone still be in the building after you left and locked up?' he asked.

'Very unlikely. There aren't any places to hide out here. And nobody but postal employees are allowed behind the counter. They would certainly have noticed someone there who didn't belong.'

'Even with the frantic rush of this last day before Christmas? Even with some temporary employees who might not know all the rules?'

'Yes, I'm sure of it.'

'But then, the murderer could be someone who had a right to be back there.'

Harold blinked and stared at Charles.

'What do you mean, Captain? One of our crew? Impossible.'

'Well, now, Harold, not really impossible.'

The lobby of the post office was a large square area. A heavy scarred table stood in the center, with a well thumbed zip code book and pens anchored to it with chains, and an ugly lamp with a green glass shade hovering over them. Everywhere else was empty space. Two walls left and right of the front doors contained numbered post office boxes and there was a door clearly marked 'Postmaster' in the far corner. Next to this door, directly opposite the front doors, the counter took up the remaining space. A few garlands were draped above the opening and a large wreath hung above it, circling the clock.

At the right of the front doors, a long table held piles of income tax forms, reminding postal patrons that as soon as the Christmas bills were paid, another bill would come due. Above this table a bulletin board held notices of federal laws concerning the post office, a few wanted posters, some of them looking yellowed and faded, and illustrations of new stamp issues.

'There's no evidence of a break-in that we can see, and no blood stains on the floor,' mused Charles. 'No sign of a scuffle either. Yet Jerome had to have been stabbed in this building. How else could he have gotten to the top of the steps, with no footprints going up?'

'I don't know, Captain, and I'm very late for Christmas Eve dinner with my family. Is there anything more you want?'

'Those front doors would have been locked from the inside, wouldn't they?'

'Yes. Tonight I locked them myself at precisely five o'clock, and everyone left by the back doors right after that.'

'And you also locked the back doors?'

'Yes, I did. At about 5:01.'

'Who else has keys to these doors?'

'Only myself and Greg, the assistant postmaster. One of us is always here to open the doors in the morning, and the doors are locked from the inside at the end of each day. A regular key is not needed for that. They have a push bar, a panic bar, that is locked with a special device so they can be locked from the inside, then no one can enter, but anyone can leave. And only our keys will open the doors from the outside.'

'No other employees have keys?'

'No. There are just the two sets. Most days the back doors are locked at five o'clock, the shade pulled down at the counter, and the front doors left open until eight o'clock, for people who want to collect their mail from their boxes. People are working in the back until then. We have a delivery from the train at six. Then the front doors are locked at eight. Today we closed up at five since there wouldn't be a train delivery tonight. A night-watchman checks periodically, as he does most of the stores around here. He checks to see if the doors are locked and if he should see any activity inside the store. I don't know if he would have been on duty tonight, but you could ask him if he saw anything out of order.'

'Good idea. Make a note of that, Perolli. Check and see if he made his rounds tonight.'

Captain Charles gazed once more around the empty lobby. Banks of post office boxes, counter with the window pulled down and hundreds of wet, dirty footprints. An impossible task to separate a murderer's footprints from the rest of the populace. He shook his head and said, 'Okay. I guess there's no more to be seen here. Thanks for your help, Harold. I'll need to get a list of the post office employees from you as soon as possible.'

'Do you really think that's necessary?' Harold growled.

'Yes, Harold, if for no other reason than to eliminate them from suspicion. And you know we have to look into every possibility.'

'Very well,' Harold snapped. 'I'll have it for you tomorrow or the next day. Tomorrow *is* Christmas, you know.'

'Sure, Harold. As soon as possible. 'Preciate it.'

Duane ushered them both out hurriedly, and made a great show of locking and testing the front doors.

'There, Captain,' he said. 'If anyone gets in here now, he's got to be small enough to get through the keyhole.'

Harold snickered at his joke, and, flipping a hand at the two policemen, hurried down the steps to his car.

'Well, Perolli,' Charles sighed, 'Might as well call it a night and go after it again after Christmas. Not much we can accomplish tomorrow. And Martha would probably leave me if I left her alone on Christmas day. Sure you won't come and have dinner with us? Martha said to try and change your mind. You know we'd be happy to have you.'

Perolli smiled and shook his head.

'Okay then. Merry Christmas, friend,' Charles said, with an affectionate punch on Perolli's shoulder.

The sergeant waved and walked on down the street to his nearby apartment. Charles got in the police car and drove home.

We Wish You a Wary Christmas

December 25, A.M.

Christmas Day dawned crisp and sunny. The snow sparkled on trees and wires, and out on the Sound, the sun shone on the water, making it look like a large mirror, reflecting all the beauty surrounding it. At Ethel Wagner's home, the family was gathered around a gigantic fir tree, decorated with silver and blue baubles, in the only room of the house large enough to contain it. The spacious living room overlooked the Sound, with windows around two sides, and the beamed ceiling showed its centuries-old beginnings.

It was a beautiful room, giving a feeling of warmth and ease. The gaily decorated tree and brightly blazing fire in the fireplace opposite the windows added to the serenity of the room. Those gathered around the tree, however, were not feeling at all serene or at ease. Thoughts of the recent death lay like a pall over the gathering, and all were trying in different ways to avoid talking about it. After presents had been opened and exclaimed over, and they were all settled in various positions with mugs of hot chocolate, Aunt Ethel said, 'Much as we all hate to, we're going to have to talk about Jerome. I doubt that any of us got much sleep last night and I know his death is on all of our minds.'

She sat on the small sofa near the fire. Lydia, in slacks and a bulky knit sweater, her long brown hair fashioned today in a sleek chignon, sat near her great-aunt on the hearth rug, with knees drawn up. Her mother sat across the room in a small barrel chair, and Judge Laurence leaned back, seemingly at ease, on the matching sofa at the other side of the fireplace.

Ethel's son sat with his wife, sprawling comfortably in a low, cushioned love seat, near his mother. David and Rose had come down from Vermont that morning to celebrate Christmas with Ethel, and were relaxing in the warmth of the fire. They were both lawyers, in practice together in a small, rural town. Ethel had, of course, told them about the murder, and now as she spoke of it, David leaned forward and said, 'Mother, you can't let this touch you. Jerome hasn't been close to any of us for many years. You know how he has lived. I'm sure there are all kinds of situations Jerome has gotten himself into that could have caused this. You know how many enemies he's made. He's done enough damage to this family and I won't have him hurting us any further!'

David thought of the coldness his cousin had shown him as they grew up together. The many, mean little tricks he had played on a young David. Jerome had been a spoiled, fat, nasty-tempered little boy, and he seemed to have grown up to be a fat, nasty adult. David grinned to himself as he remembered the revenge he and some of his friends had taken on Jerome.

Jerome had invaded their 'club house' and spitefully destroyed the model airplanes they had worked on so painstakingly, so they let him think they had hidden other projects in the shed behind David's house. When Jerome sneaked in there, he had water dumped on his head and paint splashed on his clothes. They had been grounded for a week after that prank, but it was worth it, David smiled as he remembered.

There had been other confrontations during their teenage years, but for a long time now, David had had no contact or communication of any kind with Jerome. But he had heard, through friends and through news reports, some of the things Jerome had been involved with, and had learned through the legal community that many of Jerome's dealings just missed being against the law. He was relentless in reaching his goals, and didn't seem to care how many people he ruined along the way, but he was very careful to act just within the law. As David thought of these past events, he said, 'All of us must just sit tight and wait this out. The truth will come out. I'm sure of it. And this *has* to concern something outside the family.'

'You are right, David,' Marjorie said. 'We cannot let this touch us. We know what Jerome was and what he has done. I am sorry, Ethel, and you, Lydia, but Jerome was *not* a nice person and he has done enough to hurt all of us during his life, as David says. Let us not allow his death to cause us more trouble.'

Silence fell on the little group and each retreated into his or her own thoughts. Ethel was thinking, not of her nephew Jerome, but of her husband Al, who had died many years ago. He was killed in an accident at the small fireworks factory he owned. She missed him now, as she had every day since his death and wished he could be here to help in this troubled time. Jerome was her nephew, the son of her long-dead brother. Al had always been extremely patient with Jerome's willfulness, and many times had been there to pick up the pieces and smooth things over after Jerome had gotten himself into one scrape after another, often with other young people of his acquaintance. Usually, these shenanigans were the result of Jerome's attitude that whatever he wanted should be his. The 'baby' of the family of two children, his mother had spoiled him shamelessly, and when Jerome was twelve his mother died. He grew into his teens with no authority to guide or restrain him, only an older sister who tried desperately to teach Jerome the right way to behave. He ran wild and as he grew older, he seemed to grow more and more aggressive. His exterior charm got him into the 'best' places and he used his aggression and his family's social standing to climb high in the social hierarchy. When people got to know him better, the charm that first attracted them wore thin and his destructive personality showed itself.

Lydia's thoughts were of her husband, Eric. Her father had brought her 'proof' of Eric's infidelity, pictures showing or claiming to show, Eric in compromising positions with a young lady. Harsh words followed and caused Lydia to leave Eric. She wished she could go back to that time and talk again with Eric. Since their disagreement she had come to doubt the so-called information her father had thrust before her. Eric had begun campaigning for her father's opponent in the recent election, and she knew this was her father's way of removing him from the political scene.

Lydia's mother was also thinking of Jerome's treatment of their daughter: the last straw to Marjorie. After many unhappy incidents, she had moved out of their home and left Jerome. A legal separation followed, and it had been five years since she had last spoken to her husband. It had been an unhappy marriage almost from the start. Jerome wanted a decorative hostess, a social secretary, and he also coveted her wealth. She came from a socially prominent family, originally from San Francisco. But Marjorie learned, soon after the wedding, that Jerome wasn't capable of being the loving husband she had expected, or even a friend or companion. Warmth was beyond him. He expected her to run his household efficiently, which she was quite capable of doing, but it seemed to her that any employee could have done the same. She knew she should feel grief, sorrow, something for the man she had married twenty-seven years before, but she felt nothing, not even relief.

Judge Laurence's musings went back across the years to his friendship with Al Wagner, first as college roommates and then, during World War II, when they had both served in Washington, D.C. in intelligence. They had continued this close friendship, and since Al's death forty years before, Tom Laurence had remained a staunch friend to Ethel and considered himself part of the family. He wondered now what changes this last incident might make in their relationship.

Ethel brought them all back from their wool-gathering saying, 'All of us know some secrets that must not be divulged. It could be very dangerous to all of us if these things were uncovered. I think you would all agree to that?'

'Of course, Aunt Ethel,' Lydia said, 'But what can we do?'

'We can keep our heads, answer any questions the police ask, and volunteer nothing,' David said. 'I'm sure the police will solve this murder without our help.'

'Mother, do you think we should stay with you for a few more days?' Rose asked. 'We probably should be here for the funeral.'

'Now you both have commitments. And you couldn't do any more here anyway.'

'Maybe a little moral support?' smiled Rose, glancing at David questioningly.

'Mother's right, Rose,' replied David. 'If she needs us we can get here quickly. And you know you have a court case starting soon, and I have appointments I should keep. I expect Jerome can get buried without us. He didn't really want anything to do with us when he was alive!'

Ethel frowned and shook her head.

'I'm positive you have nothing to fear, Mother,' David continued.

Judge Laurence spoke up, 'You're both right. Captain Charles is an able investigator. I'm sure he will get to the bottom of this in good time. And I will be here to do anything and everything to help.'

'We will, too, Aunt Ethel,' Lydia put in.

'Well,' Ethel said, rising purposefully. 'That's enough black thoughts on such a beautiful day. Who would like more hot chocolate?'

Captain Charles and his wife were spending a quiet Christmas Day together. After a special breakfast of Martha's famous sausage casserole, blueberry muffins and batter-fried apple slices, they were sitting next to their little Christmas tree after opening their presents to each other, both relaxing in robes and pajamas. Martha leafed through the book Charles had given her, knowing of her love of all things British – a beautiful, colorful book, *Discovering Britain and Ireland*. Smiling to herself, she thought, If only I could get him away from that job long enough to visit England, a visit he had been promising for years. She sighed and reached out to touch his hand.

'Thank you, dear. This is a lovely book. I will certainly enjoy reading it.'

Charles moved restlessly at her side. She patted his hand saying, 'Now, you are supposed to relax and forget the office just for this one day.'

Her large husband smiled at her and said, 'That's not so easy to do with this Jerome Edwards murder hanging over our heads. But for you, I'll try. What would like to do for the rest of the day?'

'What I'd like to do is simply nothing. Nothing special or planned,' Martha replied. 'I'd like us to be lazy and enjoy the peace and quiet. Can we do that? It doesn't happen very often, you know.'

Charles thought how lucky he was to have this wife. He knew he could be difficult to live with. His work kept him away from home at odd hours, and often, he brought his frustrations home with him. He would rant and complain about the pressures he was under, the politicians he had to suffer, the crimes they had no possibility of ever solving and the malice and destruction he encountered every day. But Martha took it all in her stride, kept his meals hot, listened and calmed and encouraged. Being a policeman's wife was never easy. Being this policeman's wife was hard indeed. Charles was grateful for his well ordered home and his uncomplaining helpmate. He squeezed her hand and said, 'Whatever you want, Marthie.'

Charles had been a rookie policeman when they met. Both had been halfway engaged to someone else at the time, but one evening together at a mutual friend's party, and they had no time for anyone but each other. After thirty years of marriage, they were as close as on the day of their wedding. They had been married five years when a son was born to them. They doted on the little fellow and had great plans for his future. Little Steven was a happy child, a beautiful little blue-eyed angel. And when they were told there would be no more children, they lavished all their attention on him. It was a staggering blow when, at the age of six, Stevie was diagnosed with leukemia, and after nearly a year of trying every possible treatment, the little boy died, leaving the Charles family devastated. They had seen this kind of tragedy pull other families apart, but in their case, it brought them even closer together, and though little was said, both of them thought often of their little son, even more so at Christmastime. So Martha was glad, more than ever, that Charles could spend the holiday with her, when on so many occasions she had had to spend the day alone, due to urgent police business.

For the rest of the day they read, took a long walk, played two games of Scrabble and reminisced about other Christmases. And now, with the lush harmonies of Martha's favorite Brahms Second Symphony coming from the CD player (she had declared herself weary of Christmas carols) they were trying to decide what to do about supper when the telephone rang.

'Well,' Martha sighed, as Charles got up to answer it, 'at least it has left us alone for most of the day.'

'Yes,' Charles was saying into the receiver, 'those reports

should be on my desk in the morning. Have you been able to trace his movements for the past week?'

Charles listened, nodded and made a note or two on the pad next to the telephone, and finally said, 'Okay, keep on with that. Leave me some names. And get going on those warrants as soon as possible. See you in the morning.'

Putting down the phone, he turned to Martha and said, 'They have some ideas about where Edwards has been lately, and it may help us to pin down his murderer. Sure hope it can be a break in the case.'

'I hope so too, dear,' Martha replied. 'But this is still Christmas Day. It's still *my* day. No more murder investigation, no more police station, and hopefully no more phone calls! Today you are just Mr. Charles, husband. So, what do you want for supper?'

Charles grinned, pulled Martha to her feet and said, 'Let's just eat some of that leftover stew you have in the freezer, and go to bed early.'

He hugged her to him, and, arm in arm, they headed for the kitchen.

O Come All Ye Wrathful

December 26, A.M.

At the police station, the once gay decorations were looking limp and dusty, this one day after Christmas. Charles was hard at work at his desk in the early morning. Detective Robinson, sitting in the chair next to the Captain's desk, was discussing the murder with Charles and both were leafing through papers. Perolli entered the office carrying several file folders and handed them to Captain Charles.

'This is all we've come up with since yesterday? So little to go on. But then, I guess we should be glad to have this much, with everyone busy celebrating Christmas and all.'

Charles sighed as he scanned the reports. 'Most of this is just negative stuff. I think we're going to have to go talk to some of those people Jerome had dealings with. We sure don't have much in the way of evidence.'

Perolli handed Charles a sheet of paper with a few names on it.

'Right,' said Charles, 'Let's see what we have here. Robby, maybe you can think of others that should be on this list.'

He read rapidly and began, 'Okay. Here's Mark Kovich. He was Edwards's partner, and he certainly had no love for the man. He was cheated out of his share of the partnership and swore to get even with Jerome. Course, that was years ago. Don't know of anything more recent that's happened in that affair. But we can follow up on that. Then we have Stanford Bissell. He was a friend of Jerome's but I've heard they have been at sword's points for some time. Either of you know why?'

Both shook their heads.

'Well, I guess we should find out. And we can't forget his wife, his daughter, his son-in-law and even the old judge. They all had good reason to dislike him. Not just dislike, but downright hate, after the way Jerome treated them all. All of these people I've mentioned had good reasons to really loathe him.

'Could this have been a revenge killing maybe? There was no sign of robbery or mugging. And it must have been someone he knew. No sign of a struggle that we could see, either outside where he was found, or inside the post office, where he must have come from. Just that fatal knife wound. The killer would have to have gotten close to him to stab him like that. So that should tell us it was someone he knew, or surely someone he didn't fear. Now, Edwards was involved in several organizations, Chamber of Commerce, state political groups, and he was Chairman of the Board of a couple of companies that I know of, and probably more that I don't. We can check those out and see if there have been any problems with Edwards, any problems that could lead to this. May be a long shot, but it's something to think about. Could be what? Fear? Anger? Political gain?

'We can check, too, at the newspaper office and see if anybody had a problem with him there.

'Now, the boys on duty last night were asking about Jerome's movements this past week. Seems he was seen over in Rock Falls, talking to some city types. George Adams, at the Courthouse, said he thought he knew who they were. So, we need to talk to George. One more thing to look into. Either of you have any bright ideas about the way to proceed?'

Perolli and Robinson continued to study the papers in their hands.

'There are a lot of people,' Robinson said, 'who have been burned by dealing with Edwards, besides the ones you mentioned. How about Johnny Stevens? You brought up Eric Ramsey, Edwards's son-in-law, and that reminds me of that third candidate for District Attorney. What was his name? Edwards really clobbered him, bringing up all kinds of dirt until the man was forced to pull out of the race. Edwards sure did a number on his reputation. That would sure be grounds for violence.'

'Yeah. Frank Josephs was his name. Jerome didn't pull any punches, did he? And Josephs was mighty angry. Furious even, and said so in no uncertain tones. A lot of people heard his threats to Jerome. He had to be held back from punching him after those debates, and I can't blame him for feeling the way he did. We'll add his name to the list, and anybody else you guys can think of. Now, about the sighting in Rock Falls. Seems to be the last time Jerome was seen anywhere, before he got himself killed, so we might as well start from there. Here are the names of the witnesses the boys talked to. Better get their statements and see if we can find any other people who saw Jerome in the last few days. Check on those warrants, too, will you, Robby?'

'And I want the autopsy done right away – today. Tell Doc Swenson to do it first thing. I don't care if there are bodies stacked to the ceiling in the morgue. This one has top A1 authority.'

He handed the papers to Robinson who got to his feet and sauntered out the door.

Charles shuffled the rest of the papers together and stacked them on the corner of his desk, then he said, 'Let's go, Perolli. Let's you and I start these interviews with Mr. Kovich.'

They shrugged into heavy coats, hats and mufflers. The temperature had dropped during the night and with the wind off the Sound, the windchill factor made it unpleasant to be outside for any length of time. They made their way quickly to the parking lot behind the station, and immediately turned on the heater in the car. Buckling themselves in, they headed down the Boulevard to Preston Used Cars, where Mark Kovich was a salesman, pulled into the lot and parked near the front of the sales office. Pushing through the double doors, they stomped snow from their boots and turned to face the man hurrying toward them. This was a man of average height, usually described as 'wiry', with thinning gray hair combed sidewise, as though trying to cover baldness. His complexion was pale, almost yellow, with the permanent reminders of teenage acne. He wore a polka-dot tie with his double-breasted suit, and eager smile. This smile faltered as he realized these were not potential customers.

'Greetings, gentlemen. Could I hope that you have come to replace all the city's police cars?' he said, with a wry grin.

Charles smiled and shook his head as he answered, 'No, I'm afraid not, Mark. You probably can guess why we're here. Is there someplace we can go to talk?'

'Sure. Come on in the office,' Mark said, leading the way to a small, cluttered room containing a desk completely covered with forms, brochures and sales literature. More sales posters covered the walls, showing the new, sleek models of various car manufacturers, and cartons filled with more literature were piled up against one wall. Mark sat behind the desk and gestured at the two chairs standing in the cramped space in front of the desk. Charles and Perolli sat.

Clearing his throat nervously, Mark said, 'I suppose this is about Jerome's death?' He leaned back in the swivel chair and propped one foot on an open desk drawer.

'It is,' Charles replied. 'When was the last time you talked to Edwards?'

'I'd say about three years ago, when he did the dirty on me and took the newspaper away from me.' Mark's voice shook as he went on. 'I told him then I never wanted to speak to him again, and I meant it!'

'You also said you'd pay him back, didn't you?'

'Well, for God's sake, I was angry! People say all kinds of things when they're mad. I started that paper and worked night and day, seven days a week to make it a success. Then Edwards came along, bought up shares while he was still a partner, and pushed me out! Why wouldn't I be mad? I was furious! I couldn't imagine such a thing happening. I should never have let him become my partner, if I had only known what he was like. But I needed the money for new equipment, and, of course, it was his idea for us to incorporate and sell shares in the business. He planned to take over from the very first.'

'So, you had good reason to want him dead,' Charles said.

'I certainly had cause to *wish* him dead – or any other painful calamity I could think of,' Mark said, looking down at his desk top and toying with a pencil. 'Not only did he ruin me as far as the newspaper was concerned, he ruined my life along with it. My wife left me when I lost the paper, and I lost my house 'cause I couldn't keep up the payments. Edwards left me with nothing and never looked back. But, good Lord! That was years ago. If I had it in me, I would have killed him then, I wouldn't have waited all these years.'

'Nothing has happened lately to change things between you in any way?' Charles asked.

'No. I told you, I haven't had anything to do with him in all this time. Haven't even seen him. He sure doesn't come in here! We wouldn't have anything classy enough to suit the grand exalted Mr. Edwards,' he snorted.

'That's probably true. Just for the record, Mark, would you mind telling us where you were Christmas Eve, say around 5:30 in the afternoon?' Charles asked quietly.

'Sure I can tell you. When I finished here, about five, I went to a bar. The Royal Arms. You know the place, across from the railroad station. With no one to go home to, it seemed as good a place as any to spend Christmas Eve.'

Rising, Charles said, 'Okay, Mark. I appreciate your help. If you think of anything we should know, give us a call.'

'I don't know how I could help. And I'm not sure I even want to help you catch Jerome's killer. I'd rather shake his hand or pin a medal on him. Or her. Plenty of women had it in for that louse.'

Charles turned to leave, saying, 'Think about it. Any help you can give…'

'Sure, sure. Goodbye, Captain.'

As they got in the police car, Perolli sat with his hand on the ignition key, waiting to start the car. Charles, deep in thought, with his chin on his chest, said, 'We really can't cross Mark off the list of potentials. There's sure a lot of hatred there and time doesn't always make things better. Sometimes that hatred festers into something lethal. And in Mark, there's an awful lot of bitterness dammed up, with good reason, and we only have his word that he hasn't had any contact with Jerome of late. I haven't heard of anything like that, have you?'

Perolli shook his head negatively.

'Well, I guess he'll bear watching and we will need to check his alibi for that night.'

After a few more moments, Charles straightened, reached for his seat belt and said, 'Let's go, Perolli. We'd better check out Edwards's house and see if anything there will give us a lead.'

Perolli started the car and pulled out of the used car lot.

The Folly and the Ivy

December 26, A.M.

The car moved up Beacon Hill to the imposing mansion set back from the road in a grove of trees. It spoke of wealth and care: immaculately mowed lawns and shrubs trimmed with military precision, the circular drive raked as though with a fine-toothed comb in the summertime; no leaf allowed to mar the pristine neatness in the fall, and now, in December, the snow neatly piled at the sides of the driveway and the wide steps leading to the front door swept clean of white flakes. It was a showplace. People drove by in the warm weather to view the topiary trees, clipped in the forms of birds and animals, lining the drive. The house had been featured in *Home and Garden* and attracted much attention in Sunbury and surrounding towns. This was Jerome Edwards's home, where a groundsman, chauffeur and housekeeper still lived, in quarters above the garage and in the back rooms of the house. Charles rang the doorbell and grimaced as he heard it play 'When Irish Eyes are Smiling'. The door they were facing was of a dark wood, carved into several panels, with inserts of stained glass in shades of blue and green. Long narrow windows on each side of the door were curtained in a pale green material.

In a few moments, the door was opened by Mrs. Worthington, the housekeeper for Jerome.

'Hello, Mrs. Worthington,' Charles said. 'I'm sure you have been told about Mr. Edwards's death.'

'Oh, my yes! What a terrible thing!' she said, rubbing her hands together and wiping them on her apron. 'We've talked of nothing else since we heard.'

'We've come to take a look at his papers and things. Will you show us his office, please, or his den, or wherever he took care of business?' asked Charles.

'Of course, Captain Charles. Though he didn't do much work

here at the house. I think most of his work was done at the newspaper office,' Mrs. Worthington replied, opening the door wider and motioning them into the house.

'That may be, and we'll be looking there, too. But let's see what we can find here.'

'Yes, sir. It's down this way.'

Perolli and Charles followed the housekeeper through a foyer stark in its simplicity. Black and white tiles covered the floor, and high above their heads an ornate wrought iron chandelier was suspended from the ceiling painted with geometric shapes. The only furniture in the hall was a long, narrow table, on which sat a very large Chinese vase. A wide staircase rose at one end of the hall, sweeping in a graceful curve upward until it disappeared behind an upstairs wall.

They continued through rooms, well kept, with heavy furniture polished to a dull shine, and nothing out of place. Looks almost unlived in, Charles thought as they made their way to the rear of the house. Mrs. Worthington stopped before a massive, intricately carved door. Opening it, she stood aside and said, 'This is where he might have had papers. I wasn't allowed to touch his desk, except to dust the top of it. He had me dust and vacuum in here, but I was told not to move anything, and I did just like he said.'

'Is there anywhere else in the house he could have had papers? Personal papers, or business papers?' Charles asked.

'No, I don't think so. At least I've never seen anything like that anywhere else. And I would have seen it, I think. He did like to keep everything tidy.'

'Thank you, Mrs. Worthington. We'll let you know if we need anything else,' Charles said, dismissively.

The housekeeper bobbed her head and left the doorway.

Charles walked into the room and stopped before an antique desk, placed in front of floor to ceiling bookcases, covering an entire wall. He went behind the desk and sat in the cushioned desk chair, running his palms over the carving on its arms.

'Pretty nice, eh, Perolli?'

A small step stool stood before the bookcases. Perolli climbed up a step and ran his fingers over the bindings of history, philosophy and classical literature, as well as biography and current fiction and poetry. An eclectic collection, much of it looking unread, the rich leather bindings giving the impression of books possessed for their value, rather than for the education or enjoyment of their owner. Perolli thought of his own much smaller library: books that were old friends worn from many readings.

Near the windows, a large standing globe of the world filled the corner. All of the furniture in the room was of heavy, dark wood, except for a comfortable-looking maroon leather chair with its matching ottoman, taking up space in the corner opposite the windows, with a piecrust table next to it. On the table was a book, marked with a tooled leather bookmark, as though Jerome had been sitting there reading. Perolli strolled over and leaned close without touching the book, to read its title. *Business and Industry 1900–1945* he read.

Over the chair was a hanging lamp, with a tiffany glass shade. A credenza with glass doors occupied most of the remaining wall space, and on the shelves sat statuary and porcelain, antique snuff boxes and what looked to Charles's untrained eye to be a bronze Remington of an Indian on a horse.

The rug was deep purple, thick and soft. Their footsteps were well muffled as they moved about the room. Brocade drapes in a variety of shades of purple, from palest lavender to darkest mauve, covered the windows, reaching almost to the ceiling and falling to the floor. The drapes were open and they could see a park-like area behind the house. Trees, bare of leaves now in the winter, would make a pleasant vista in the spring and summer months and a brilliant splash of color in the fall.

As Charles turned his attention to the desk, he tried the drawers and discovered they were all locked.

'I'm not surprised, after what Mrs. Worthington said. He didn't trust anyone, did he! Hope one of these keys of Jerome's will fit the lock.'

He pulled a key ring from his pocket, tried the smallest one in the lock of the middle drawer and was successful in opening it.

'Okay, Perolli, let's see what we have here. Make a list of everything we find,' Charles said as he began opening one drawer after another.

'Aha. Good. A coupla bank books, and a bank statement. A recent one, dated December 15.'

Perolli leaned over Charles's shoulder, notebook in hand.

'Bills, statements, invoices, newspaper clippings, real estate brochures. Looks like Mrs. Worthington was right. He didn't do much business from here. All this looks like personal stuff. This bank book looks interesting. Look here. Every month five thousand dollars was deposited. Wonder where that came from. Stocks? Investments? All these other amounts are different. Suppose that means anything?'

Perolli shrugged, picked up the bank statement and placed it in front of Charles.

'Wow! He did pretty well for himself, didn't he! You know, another thing we have to find out is who inherits all this, plus the newspaper and lots more. Have to talk to his lawyer. And there's a safe deposit key on the key ring. Have to check that out, too.'

Charles continued to leaf through the items pulled from the desk drawers. 'Now here's something that might help,' he said, handing an address book to Perolli. 'We'll need to check out all these names. And here's his calendar. Let's see.'

Charles leaned back in the chair and flipped through the pages, stopping at December 18. 'Dental appointment. And on these other dates, mostly just initials. We'll check them with the address book. Hmm. Two days before he died, here's 'dinner-C' then 'V-C'. Interesting. Wonder what that means? Any V.C. in the address book?'

Perolli turned pages then shook his head.

'Not a thing here on the day he died or the day before. That's sort of curious in itself. Every other page has something written in. I hope we can track him for those few days. His activities then might have had something to do with his getting killed. He's been mistreating people for years. There must have been some event, some incident that triggered this. Well, we can take all this along with us and get the boys busy on it. Doesn't seem to be much more of interest here. He sure didn't keep much around, did he! I'll get a crew over to look through the rest of the house.'

Bundling the papers and books together and picking up the

keys, Charles stood and started to leave the room, then stepped back and picked up the real estate folders.

'May not mean anything, but it is curious. Wonder what sort of property he was planning to buy or invest in?'

He turned at the door and glanced around the room with appreciation.

'This sure is a beautiful room, isn't it! Bet that stuff in the cupboards is worth a pretty penny. Someone's going to have a great time cataloging and maybe auctioning off all these things. And this is only one room. Just think how much more there is to dispose of. Guess a lot will depend on what his will says. Boy, there's got to be a fortune here!'

Retracing their steps to the front of the house, they met Mrs. Worthington in the foyer. With her was the chauffeur, Buck Riley, and a young woman the housekeeper introduced as her niece, Flora.

'Flora has been helping me out here, and we were wondering,' Mrs. Worthington said haltingly, 'What are we to do? Should we stay here and keep up the house? We're paid to the end of the month, but then what should we do?'

'We'll be getting in touch with Mr. Edwards's lawyer, and we'll let you know, or he will,' Charles answered. 'In the meantime, why don't you just go on as usual until we know more. Anyway,' Charles said with a smile, 'When his will is read, you may all be rich!'

'Hah!' snorted Buck. 'That'll be the day! Couldn't afford a kind word to any of us when he was alive!'

'Now, Buck,' Mrs. Worthington tittered nervously, 'You shouldn't be saying things like that.'

'Why not? Ask anyone who ever worked for him. Meanest man around,' said Buck. 'I've been working for him a long time, and for over a month I've been asking for some extra time off. He told me if I took off, I didn't need to come back. He's been hassling me a lot lately.'

'How do you mean?' Charles asked.

'Oh, complaining about the way the cars were kept. Telling me I was late picking him up, when I was there exactly when he told me to be. Stuff like that.'

'More so than usual?'

'Maybe a little, but then he always did have a short fuse.'

'Know any reason why he should be more critical of late?'

'Beats me.'

Buck Riley was a big man, over six feet tall, with a barrel chest and well muscled arms. He reminded Charles of one of those wrestlers on TV, Gorgeous George or others of his ilk. If he wanted to kill his employer, thought Charles, It wouldn't be with a knife. Just one blow with those hands would do it.

'Have you noticed anything unusual lately? Anything different from Mr. Edwards's regular schedule?' Charles asked the housekeeper. 'Do you know if he has gotten any threats? Has he seemed nervous or afraid?'

Mrs. Worthington shook her head.

'Everything has been normal, Captain,' the housekeeper said. 'Actually, we didn't see him a lot. Mr. Edwards spent most of the day away from the house. I fixed his breakfast, then most days I wouldn't see him again until the next morning. Sometimes he was here for dinner, but most of the time he ate out, at his club or somewhere I think. He'd leave me a note on the hall table if he expected to be home for a meal. And then, of course, there were times when he had people here for dinner, but then it was planned way ahead of time, and usually he had other people come in and help with the cooking and serving. He used to have dinner parties quite a lot when the Missus was still here.'

'How about you, Buck? Have you noticed anything different? Any change in his attitude, besides what you just said?'

'No. It's the same with me,' Buck said. 'He doesn't – didn't – always want me to drive him places. I take care of all the cars, but a lot of the time he liked to drive himself. Used the Mercedes. A real sweet car.'

'And you don't have any idea why he's been on you lately?'

'No idea. I haven't done anything any different than what I usually do.'

'How long has he been hassling you?'

'Oh, I suppose most of the last month.'

'How long have you worked here, Buck?'

'About five years. It was just him living here when I first

started working for him.'

'And your job is pretty much full time? You have to be here and ready in case he needs you?'

'That's it. I never could be sure when he might expect me to take him somewhere.'

'And you, Mrs. Worthington. How long have you been working here?'

'I've been housekeeper here for fourteen years come next March. Little Lydia was only about ten years old when I first came to work for Mr. and Mrs. Edwards. I felt really sad to see both of them go. Lydia and Mrs. Edwards I mean.'

'So you've known the family for a long time. Do you have any ideas at all about who might have killed Mr. Edwards?'

'No, I really don't. I know he was a very impatient man, and he surely made people mad at him,' Mrs. Worthington replied.

'How did you feel about him?'

'How did I feel?'

'Yes. Did you like him?'

'I won't say I really liked him, no. He could be very abrupt and demanding and could get in a rage over such little things, so you never quite knew where you were with him. He didn't seem to care to get close to anyone. I guess mostly I felt sorry for him, being here alone and all, though I'm sure it was his own fault. But then, this was a good job. He paid well.'

'He paid well, but expected a lot for his money, I guess,' Charles said.

They both nodded in agreement.

'Okay. If either of you think of anything we ought to know, please call the station.'

As he gingerly shook Buck's hand and nodded to the two women, Charles said, 'We'll be getting in touch soon, and a crew from the police station will be here to go through the rest of the house. Thanks for your help.'

With a wave of his hand, Perolli followed Charles down the curving front walk to the police car.

'Funny sort of place, isn't it, Perolli,' Charles said. 'More like a museum or a fancy hotel than a home.'

He stopped at the car and gazed around.

'While we're out here, maybe we ought to talk to some of his neighbors. That house over there. Isn't that where the Cochran sisters live?'

Perolli nodded, put the car keys back in his pocket and followed Charles across the street.

The house across from the Edwards mansion was in sharp contrast to the imposing one they had just left. A small Cape Cod cottage, it looked homey and welcoming, with starched, ruffled curtains showing in the front windows, and a flower box filled with greenery and red plastic poinsettias next to the front steps. Low bushes made a frame around the front of the house and two trees, one on each side, stood like sentinels guarding the property and holding down the corners of the lot. The house was painted white and blue shutters enclosed the many-paned windows.

Charles had hardly touched the doorbell when the door was flung open and two tiny people met his eyes. They wore identical cotton print dresses, gray cardigan sweaters and 'sensible' low-heeled brown shoes. Each had her hair twisted into a bun high on her head. Chubby, but spry, was the description that came to Charles's mind as they greeted the men with delight. Visitors were rare and they were excitedly anticipating this visit.

'Come in! Oh, do come in, my dear Anthony and Douglas,' said one of the women. Miss Charlotte, Charles recalled. Both women had been school teachers in the local grammar school. Charles felt that it had been about two centuries ago, but admitted to himself that it was closer to forty years. As a matter of fact, both had taught Captain Charles and Perolli. One, Miss Charlotte, in the first grade, and the other, Miss Norma, in the second grade. So they felt a little like those two small boys now, as they faced these two former teachers.

'Oh, do come into the parlor. It's not often we have two handsome gentleman callers,' Miss Norma giggled, and Miss Charlotte tittered with her.

With a great deal of fussing, the men were finally settled in what the elderly ladies called their front parlor, where every chair wore a lacy, starched antimacassar, and little tables were scattered around the room, seemingly haphazardly. A small Christmas tree sat on one table, decorated with strings of popcorn and cranberries and ornaments that surely could be considered antiques.

Seating himself on an uncomfortable horsehair sofa, that must have been around since the war – the Civil War – Charles began, 'We're investigating the death of Jerome Edwards.'

'I knew it! I told you, Charlotte, that that was why they were over there in that house!'

'Yes, you did. And remember, I said, "Wouldn't it be fun if they came over here to talk to us?"'

'You did! You did. And here they are. But what do you suppose they want from us?'

'Ladies! Ladies!' gasped Charles, trying to stem the flow of this dialogue. 'We won't stay long but...'

'Would you like some lemonade?' asked Norma.

'Oh, stay as long as you want,' said Charlotte.

'Or some cookies?' asked Norma. 'We only just finished baking a batch of ginger snaps.'

'Those are our favorites. The recipe is one that has been handed down from our grandmama,' Charlotte said.

'No, no,' Charles put in hastily. 'We just wanted to ask if you had seen anything at Mr. Edwards's house that might help us solve this crime.'

The little ladies looked at each other, and Charlotte said, 'We really don't see much going on over there.'

'And we weren't very friendly with Mr. Edwards.'

'Now, Norma, that's not quite true. *He* wasn't very friendly with *us*.'

'You're right, Charlotte. He was a mean person. Oh, we tried to be good neighbors, didn't we, Charlotte, when he first moved there. That was the old Johnson place, you know.'

'Hector Johnson, whose family owned the sand banks.'

'Of course, Mr. Edwards changed a lot in the house and in the grounds after he bought it. It hardly looks like the same place.'

'But he didn't like our cats,' said Norma.

'Your cats,' Charles said, trying to follow their leaps from one subject to another.

'Yes, we have three little kitties, and they wander. Well, of course they do. Cats are curious, and one can't keep them penned up.'

Right on cue, as though they were aware they were being talked about, two Siamese blue points stalked into the room, tails erect like little furry flags. They sniffed disdainfully at Perolli's boots, glanced in Charles's direction, then lost interest and sprawled bonelessly near the window, in a square of sunlight. Lying in a welter of legs, it was hard to tell where one cat began and the other ended. A third cat, a small calico, poked its head around the door frame, then quickly withdrew and disappeared.

The ladies smiled fondly at the cats.

'That's Napoleon and Josephine,' Charlotte said, pointing to the two Siamese.

'And the dear little calico is Angel,' Norma added. 'Aren't they sweet?'

'Uh, yes,' Charles said. 'Now about Mr. Edwards?' he prompted.

'Mr. Edwards? What about him?' Charlotte asked.

'Mr. Edwards and your cats?'

'Oh, yes,' Norma said. 'When our kitties wandered over into Mr. Edwards's yard, he kicked them! Can you imagine such a terrible thing!'

Both women glared in the direction of the house across the street, and Charlotte continued, 'Well, we saw him and we just went right over there.'

'Yes, we did. We told him he should not treat these poor little pussycats that way,' said Norma.

'And do you know what he said?'

'He said if he caught them in his yard again, he would wring their necks!'

'Awful man!' Both ladies looked distressed as they remembered this experience.

Brightening, Miss Norma said, 'But that nice Mr. Bissell smiled at us and told us he was sorry.'

'Mr. Bissell? Stanford Bissell? He was at Edwards's house?' asked Charles in surprise. He glanced at Perolli with raised eyebrows.

'Oh, yes,' Charlotte said. 'We've seen him several times going into the house.'

'He never stays long,' put in Norma.

'No,' Charlotte said, 'Not long at all. Only a matter of a few minutes.'

'How often has he been there?' Charles asked.

'Oh, probably about once a month, don't you think, Norma?' Charlotte answered.

'Why, yes,' Norma replied. 'Always on the day we bundle up our newspapers for recycling.'

'Why, that's right. We would see him when we took our bundles of newspapers out to the curb to be picked up.'

'It's so important to recycle as much as possible, don't you think?' said Norma. 'We put out our glass and plastic, too. Not that we have a whole lot of it, but every little bit helps.'

'If everyone did that, it would save a lot. Just think of the number of trees…'

'Yes, of course, ladies,' Charles put in quickly, before the conversation could get sidetracked again. 'So that would be once each month?'

Both women nodded. 'Always on the first Monday,' Norma added.

'Is there anything else you can think of, Miss Norma, Miss Charlotte, that you might have seen or heard across the street that might throw some light on this investigation?' asked Charles.

'No,' Charlotte answered. 'About the only people we see over there are the gardener, or whatever he's called, and the house-keeper and one of the big cars coming and going,' Charlotte said.

'And, of course, we see delivery trucks, and once in a while a repair truck.'

'Yes, remember? Norma, there was a plumber's vehicle there just last week.'

'Then, once in a blue moon, there are other cars and lots of lights as though there is a party going on.'

'But not very often, Charlotte,' Norma said.

'No, not very often, but it does happen,' Charlotte said.

'It used to happen quite a lot,' Norma said. 'How long do you think it has been since they had big parties there?'

Charles stood hurriedly and motioned to Perolli, who put away his notebook and moved toward the door.

'Thank you, ladies. If we think of anything you might help us with, we'll come back and see you,' Charles said.

The Misses Cochran giggled at this, and said, almost in unison, 'Oh, please do come back!'

As they got into the police car, Charles chuckled, 'I think those two are the only people who call us by our first names. Makes you feel as though you were back in the first grade, doesn't it! And you know, I think if anything at all important happened across the street from them, those women would have seen it. They don't miss much, do they! Do you suppose they take turns watching out the windows, just in case they might miss something? I guess that's their only amusement, bless their hearts. I wonder what they talk about all day long to each other. Probably use two hundred words just commenting on the weather!

'But that's really a strange thing about Stanford Bissell being over there so much. Wonder what that's all about. I thought they weren't on speaking terms. It's another puzzle, one more thing we have to look into.'

Charles chuckled then and said, 'Wouldn't it be a riot if we found out those two stabbed Edwards because he kicked their cats!'

He's Making a List and Checking it Twice…

December 26, A.M.

On the way back to the police station, Charles said, 'I keep thinking about that door in the post office. No one seems to know anything about it, or at least, they *say* they don't. A little strange, don't you think? That still bothers me. And, you know, that's where Edwards's footprints start, at the top of the stairs, only outside. Why don't you see what you can find out, Perolli. Try to locate the original plans for the building. Ought to be in the planning office. Maybe you can think of another place to look. But I think it's a very important piece of information that we need to solve this thing.'

Perolli nodded his assent, dropped Charles off at the station and headed back toward the center of town.

Meanwhile, Charles sat at his desk and made lists of all the people he could think of who were connected to Jerome in any way, and their difficulties with him. At the top of the list he wrote:

Mrs. Marjorie Edwards – Separated from her husband, and hated the man.

Below that he noted:

Mrs. Lydia Ramsey   – Father ruined her marriage.
Mr. Eric Ramsey   – Same motive.

Continuing the list he added:

Mark Kovich   – Jerome cheated him out of the newspaper he had founded, and he swore to get even.

Stanford Bissell	– Bad feelings noted, but why? Why was he visiting Edwards regularly, according to the Cochran sisters?

'C' in Edwards's date book???

Buck Riley	– Jerome antagonistic toward him of late. Why? J. afraid of Buck? What other reason?
Johnny Stevens	– Past injury.
Frank Joseph	– J. ruined his reputation in the campaign for D.A. Threatened J.

Editor Paul Brady, newspaper employees???

Scratching his head, Charles leaned back in his chair, thinking of others he could add to the list. Pretty short list, he thought, For a man so universally hated. He surely made enemies when he ran – and lost – the campaign for District Attorney, and he was constantly stirring up hornet's nests through his newspaper. Editorials that he wrote spewed venom machine-gun style. Didn't seem to care who got hurt.

But Charles couldn't recall anything recent that could have stirred up enough hate (or panic) to lead to murder.

He looked up from his reading as the door opened and Perolli came in with a set of blueprints under one arm. Smiling, he laid them on the Captain's desk and began to unroll them.

'Great! Are these the architect's plans for the post office building?'

Perolli nodded. Charles helped him anchor the sides of the blueprints with a coffee mug on one corner and a stapler on the other. Perolli added books to hold down the other corners.

Charles stared at the plans, tracing lines with a blunt finger.

'There's the front door. No, this is. Damn, these things aren't easy to read, are they! There!' Stabbing the plans with his forefinger, Charles leaned over and peered nearsightedly at the blueprints. 'Can't quite make it out – Oh, thanks,' he said, as Perolli handed him his glasses.

'All right. Now I see what it is.' Pointing to the lines showing an opening in the exterior of the building, he shouted, 'It's a small room, and look here! There's a door going from this room to the outside. Darned if I ever noticed it from the outside. Did you?'

Perolli shook his head and continued to study the plans.

'Look over here. There's another door just like that one on the other side of the front doors. Didn't Duane mention something about a closet there? But I don't see an outside door for that one. It would be pretty silly to have a door going outside from a closet, don't you think? Never heard of such a thing. Actually, it seems an odd way to build wouldn't you say? Especially a post office, a government building. They would have to be extra careful of security and such. Of course, it's an old building, and maybe security wasn't so important then. And with the two sets of doors into the building, these doors, or rooms, or closets, make the outside walls flush. I'm sure that's why we never noticed. And maybe that's why it was built this way. And like I say, it's an old building and maybe there was some use for these rooms back when it was built, then during the years they just got forgotten and unused.

'And you know that has to be where Jerome was stabbed. But how did he – how did *they* – get into that room? And as far as that goes, how did they get into the building at all? No one we've talked to knows anything about the little room, at least no one has admitted knowing about it. We've got to find out who could have had a key to the building. Sort of puts us back to the people who work at the post office, who could still have been in the building after the place was locked up.

'Have we got the names of the postal employees from Duane yet?'

Perolli shook his head.

'Well, we will have to talk to Duane again. Make a note to give him a call. And let's find out who might have worked there in the past, too. Maybe someone who was fired, somebody who would have a beef with Edwards. Lord knows he was always sticking his nose in places he didn't belong.

'And I'm still not crossing Harold Duane off our list of suspects.'

Charles reached under the blueprints and pulled out the list he had been working on, running his eyes down the names.

'None of these people would have had a way to get into the post office building,' he said.

He shoved the list at Perolli. After a moment, Perolli pushed the paper back, with a finger on one name.

'What?' Charles asked. 'Stanford Bissell? How could he... Hey! You're right! He was Postmaster seven or eight years ago, wasn't he! That was just before I came back here. Good work, Perolli. I think we have another visit to make. We have other things to ask Mr. Bissell, too.'

Rolling up the blueprints and stuffing them into his desk drawer, he grabbed his coat from the coat rack and headed for the parking lot, with Perolli trailing behind him.

...Gonna Find Out Who's Naughty or Nice...

December 26, A.M.

Marjorie Edwards lived in a compact, ranch-type house in a relatively new housing development on the outskirts of Sunbury. Since her separation from Jerome she had lived here alone, until the break-up of Lydia's marriage, when Lydia moved in with her. Lydia's days were spent at her job as proofreader in a local print shop, and Marjorie spent her time with bridge-playing, shopping and luncheon dates with her widowed or divorced friends. She was pulling on gloves in the front hallway when the front doorbell sounded. With a little moue of annoyance, she went to the door. Her annoyance vanished when she found Eric standing on the porch.

'Oh, Eric! Come in! I am glad to see you,' she said.

Eric hesitated and said, 'I wasn't sure of my welcome, but I had to come talk to you.'

He ducked his head to enter the doorway, a habit of his, as he was well over six feet tall. He was neatly dressed in a gray turtleneck sweater, darker gray slacks, a navy overcoat and black ankle boots. He was bareheaded and a shock of dark, unruly hair fell over his forehead as he shook off some snow. Eric was a pleasant-looking young man, clean-shaven, with deep brown, wide-spaced eyes, eyes that now looked apprehensive. His mouth was a little over-large, but since it was usually smiling, it could not be considered a physical drawback. He smiled now, as Marjorie led the way down two steps into the sunken living room. She indicated a chair, and sat in its twin, saying, 'I am very glad to see you, Eric. I want you to know that I never believed the crimes Jerome accused you of.'

'I sure am glad to hear you say that,' sighed Eric. 'Now if I can only convince Lydia.'

'Give her some time, Eric. I think she disbelieved the evidence also, but you know her pride.'

Ruefully Eric said, 'Pride is what got us both into this mess. I was angry because she didn't believe me...'

'And even if she changed her mind, she had too much stubborn pride to admit it,' finished Marjorie. 'Yes, how well I know. In that respect she is very like her father.'

'Well, I had to come and talk to you, hopefully to both of you, to see if I can't get us back together. You know that I still love her and I've wanted so many times to come to see her. Each time I was stopped by that dumb pride, and afraid she wouldn't see me. But now that her father is gone, maybe she will listen.'

'We can only hope that this crime is solved soon, and we can all go on with our lives. Perhaps it will be better for all of us,' said Marjorie.

'I hope so,' Eric said. 'May I come back when Lydia is home? Do you think she will see me?'

'I will certainly speak to her and try to convince her that a reconciliation is best for both of you.'

'You know why Mr. Edwards did what he did, don't you?' asked Eric.

'Of course. You were in his way when he was running for the office of District Attorney, and you had to be removed from the game. It is only unfortunate that he could not think of his daughter's happiness instead of his lust for power.' Marjorie's eyes snapped and her mouth formed a thin line. 'I am very sorry this had to happen, Eric, but I feel sure that everything will work out now for the best.'

Eric stood and said, 'You must have been on your way someplace. I shouldn't keep you any longer.'

'I was just leaving, but you did not make me late,' Marjorie said, as she ushered Eric to the front door. 'And even if you had made me late, it would have made no difference. I am so happy you came. Come back tomorrow evening. Lydia will be here and I shall insist that she stay and talk to you.'

'Thank you, Mrs. Edwards,' said Eric. 'I really appreciate your help.'

'You are quite welcome, Eric. I think it might be a good idea anyway, if we all stayed close, presenting a united front, as it were.

You know all of us could be considered suspects in Jerome's murder,' she said.

'Yes, I'm aware of that,' Eric replied. 'But since we're innocent, we should have no problems there.'

'Don't count on it. Jerome's malice could reach us, even now,' she snapped.

A look of alarm passed over Eric's face, but he said calmly, 'I know it will all turn out okay. I'll see you both tomorrow night. Would around 7:30 be a good time?'

'Yes, that would be fine. We will be waiting for you. Goodbye, Eric.'

The Captain and his Sergeant waved to the owner of the diner, their customary place for lunch, as they seated themselves at the counter. Charles picked up the newspaper lying there.

'The usual, Jerry,' he said.

'Comin' right up, guys,' Jerry responded.

In a short time he placed a cheeseburger and an order of French fries in front of Charles and poured him a cup of coffee. A bowl of vegetable soup and a glass of milk was set down at Perolli's place. Perolli raised his eyebrows at Charles's lunch.

'Don't start, Perolli,' Charles said, taking a large bite of his sandwich. 'So my blood pressure and cholesterol are up. A man has to have some pleasures. And you don't need to go telling Martha what I eat.'

The owner of the diner leaned on the counter in front of them and asked, 'Anything new on the murder?'

'"Fraid not, Jerry. We're just slogging along, trying to get things pieced together. You didn't know the man, did you?'

'Only by reputation. He would hardly have graced this establishment with his high and mighty presence, now would he?' Jerry grinned.

'Probably not. Among other things he was a bit of a snob, I gather.'

'You could say that. Didn't know anyone who was in Mr. Edward's circle either, but I assume they were the cream of society?'

'Yeah,' Charles laughed. 'From things we hear, he must have

been the curdled cream of society. And I'm sure you and I just weren't in his league.'

Other customers arrived and Jerry reluctantly moved on down the counter to serve them. Charles went back to perusing the newspaper, chuckling at the cartoons and frowning at the editorials as he made quick work of his cheeseburger.

Finishing their lunch, the two policemen buckled themselves into the police car and soon were speeding down the Boulevard heading for Stanford Bissell's home in Salem Estates. Bissell was an accountant, and worked out of his home, so they were reasonably confident of finding him home.

They parked the car at the curb in front of the house, or as close as possible with all the snow piled up by the snowplows. This was a working-class neighborhood. Most of the front walks and driveways had been cleared of snow, and Christmas decorations still adorned the porches, bushes and even some roofs. A Santa Claus, complete with reindeer and sleigh and bag of toys romped across the roof of the house next to Bissell's. Stanford's house was bare of decoration, and as they walked up the ramp to the front door, they thought of Mrs. Bissell, injured in an automobile accident several years before. The house had been remodeled to accommodate her wheelchair, with everything on one floor, and this ramp making easy access to the driveway. Bissell answered their knock and stood back to let them in the house.

'Mr. Bissell,' Charles said, 'May we talk to you for just a minute? We won't take too much of your time. We know you're probably busy.'

'I'm not too busy right now. I don't have any appointments until this afternoon, and this time of the year is not too bad.' Stanford replied. 'But the closer we get to April 15, the busier I get.'

'That's something I'd rather not be reminded of,' Charles said with a mock shudder.

As the three men settled in chairs in the living room, Charles began, 'We've come to ask you some questions about your relationship to Jerome Edwards, in the hope that you might shed some light on this crime.'

If asked to describe Stanford Bissell, most people would say 'average'. Medium height. Medium build. Medium brown hair. Nothing outstanding about his features except for a droopy mustache and very dark, piercing eyes. He blinked now, behind steel-rimmed spectacles and said, 'My relationship with Jerome ended some time ago. We once were friends, and now we are not. That's all you need to know.'

'I've been told you had what we might call a falling out a few years ago,' Charles said.

'That is so. So it would have nothing to do with his death. It was quite a long time ago.'

Stanford sat back and placed his fingertips together, tapping them with a nervous movement.

'Then tell me, Mr. Bissell,' Charles said quietly, 'Why have you been seen visiting Jerome at his home several times lately?'

Stanford started and sat up jerkily. After a moment he smiled wryly and said, 'The Misses Cochran I suppose.'

'Doesn't matter where we heard it. Why have you been seeing Jerome if, as you say, you are no longer friends?'

'That is a personal matter, and I don't have to answer you,' Bissell snapped.

'If we find that it has a bearing on the case, we can insist that you tell us,' Charles said. After a moment, when Bissell failed to respond, he added, 'Something else had come up that we thought you might help us with. You were Postmaster here in Sunbury seven or eight years ago, weren't you?'

'Why, yes. I was.' Bissell nervously fingered his bow tie and seemed startled at this turn in the questioning.

'We found a little room in the post office, just off the lobby, at the left of the front doors. Do you know anything about it?'

'Why, now that you mention it, there is a door there. But I was told it was just empty space,' Bissell said in surprise. 'So I never gave it a second thought.'

'Why would there be a door there if it was just empty space?'

'I'm sure I wouldn't know, Captain. I never questioned it.'

'You didn't have a key to that door?'

'No, of course not. I told you I didn't even think about it.'

'Do you still have keys to the post office doors?'

'Certainly not! Any keys I had were turned over to the new man, Harold Duane, when he took my place. I had to sign several forms saying I had given them to him. Postal regulations. If you're looking for someone who could have gotten into the post office and also had it in for Jerome, talk to Duane! Jerome was trying to get him fired from his job, just like he...' Bissell stopped and clamped his mouth shut.

'Just like he used his influence to get *you* replaced. We thought that might be the case. I'm sure that could be one reason your friendship with Edwards ended. Though I believe you were still working on committees together after that.'

Charles waited, but again getting no response, he continued, 'We'll be sure to talk to Harold again at any rate. By the way, I've heard you have been selling quite a bit of your property lately. Why is that?'

'If it's any of your business, Captain,' growled Bissell, 'the expenses of nursing for my wife have been growing and I needed the money. I can't see that this is any of your business either.'

'Maybe not. Maybe not. Just curious is all. If you change your mind and want to tell us about your problems with Edwards, let us know. By the way, where were you on Christmas Eve, say around 5:30?'

'I was right here, Captain,' Bissell replied. 'With my wife. The nurse had left earlier and I was getting dinner started. That satisfy you?'

'Yep. Fine. That's all we needed to ask you. But we may want to talk to you again.'

Bissell stood as Charles and Perolli retrieved their hats and left the house.

He stared after them, clenching and unclenching his fists. As the car left he ran his hands through his hair and dropped into a chair.

Back in the car, Charles glanced back at the house and said, 'You know, it's funny that he would get all upset about our knowing of his visits with Edwards. Nothing really illegal about that. And that property thing. Those were expensive lots he sold. And from all I've heard, there's very little nursing to be done for his wife. The county nurse comes in twice each week and a cleaning lady once a week. Other than that, my wife tells me Mrs. Bissell does very well getting around the house in her wheelchair. Martha has known Mrs. Bissell for a long time. I think they used to play canasta with a group of women before Mrs. Bissell's accident. Have to ask Martha again what she knows about the situation.

'That accident was really sad. Mrs. B. was just getting started as a dance teacher and, of course, the accident ended all that. I remember when it happened. Did anyone ever get charged in the smash-up?'

Perolli shook his head.

'Yeah, right, I think I do remember. The other driver was fined for driving with a suspended license. Seems I also remember there was something strange about the accident, some doubt about who was really driving the car. Don't know if it has anything to do with this case, but remind me to look it up. See if we have anything new on the accident.'

Charles was silent as the car moved away from the house. After a time he said, 'Then Stanford says he hasn't had anything to do with Jerome in years. So why has he been at Jerome's house? Once a month is pretty regular. What if they were in some sort of business together? It would have to be a very secret deal, no one seems to have heard of anything like that. But what other reason could he have for calling at Edwards's house? Especially since he says he can't stand the man. What about a business deal gone sour? That would be another good motive for murder. We don't seem to lack for good motives, do we!'

Both were lost in thought as they drove back up Central Drive. Then Charles said, 'Perolli, drop me at the newspaper office, then see if you can verify these people's alibis. Find out if the people we have questioned really were where they say they were. I'll see you back at the station.'

I Wonder As I Wander

December 26, P.M.

Entering the building housing *The Reporter*, Charles stopped at the desk of the perky young receptionist, Mary Harley.

'Hi, Captain Charles,' she said, dimpling. 'What can we do for you today?'

'Can I just stay here and look at you? I haven't seen many smiling faces lately,' he joked.

'Oh, Captain, you're such a tease!'

'What I really need is to see your editor. Is he available?'

'I'm sure he is. Go right on through. You know where his office is,' Mary replied.

'Thanks, Mary.'

Charles made his way past desks and teletype machines and clattering typewriters. He could hear the slam of presses off to his right. Paul Brady's office was in the corner of the big room. As he approached, Paul waved and beckoned him in, the telephone to his ear. Charles sat in the only chair in the room, as Paul finished his phone conversation. Putting down the telephone, Paul said, 'I'm glad to see you. Saves me a trip to your place. What can you tell me about this murder?'

'Not much. With murder, the first thing we look for is evidence at the scene. Edwards's body and his footprints are all we have to go on there. Nothing else. No murder weapon, no chance of fingerprints, nobody dropped his wallet or left his calling card. It's as though Jerome was there all alone. So then we have to go to motive. Who would have hated or feared him enough to kill him?

'Well, you know as well as I that where we had nothing to go on in the first place, we have all kinds of suspects when we talk about motive. I don't have to tell you how this man was disliked. We've talked to people and we'll talk to a lot more. I can't tell you who we've been to see, but you could probably guess. But so far, no real leads.'

'No leads at all?' Paul asked.

'Nothing concrete. Just adding facts and theories until we can put some of it together. But what I came to see you about... Paul, we've been friends for a long time, and I'm going to ask a favor of you. I need to see what's in Jerome's office. Do I need to get a warrant for that?'

'The newspaper was owned by Jerome,' Paul replied, 'But I guess I'm in charge now. At least for the present. So come on, let's both go see what's in there.'

Paul, an energetic, rather untidy man, always seeming to be in motion, even when sitting down, jumped up and walked quickly to the hallway behind his office and opened the door at the end.

'Didn't often get back here,' he laughed. 'This was the inner sanctum. Commands were issued from here, demands came from here, but mostly in the form of intercom and telephone and inter-office memo. Actually, we didn't see much of him. Came in to write his editorials, and didn't mingle with the "little people". We sometimes joked that his editorials should be printed on asbestos. That's how hot they were! And we weren't allowed to change a single word, or even a comma. One of the young, innocent proofreaders did once – she was a college English major – and she was gone before the smoke cleared. Interesting man, he was.'

'That's the kindest thing anyone has said about him yet,' Charles laughed.

'He sure did put the fear of God into people,' Paul said cheerfully.

'At least you don't seem to have been afraid of him. He wasn't after you, the way I've heard he was of many others.'

'No. We got along okay. I just mostly stayed out of his way. He had a lot of investigations going, though,' Paul said.

'Like what?'

'Let's see. He had people looking into the new highway that's supposed to go through here, and he was checking out the new District Attorney. Had several people checking his background. Of course, that could just be spite. After all, Jerome did lose the election, and he never did take losing very well.

'He was running editorials on the police department, too,'

Paul chuckled. 'You might have been out job hunting if he kept that up. He wasn't very happy with you people. What did you do? Give him a parking ticket?'

Charles grinned. 'I'm not sure what we did to annoy him. It didn't take much to rile the man. What else was he checking into?'

'Oh, he was always digging into something. Even had me looking up stuff on the fireworks factory accident.'

'You mean the one that killed his uncle? But that was years ago.'

'Hey, time didn't mean anything to Edwards. He was digging up stuff about the hospital fire. That was a long time ago, too. And the bridge that collapsed over in Port Haven. Seemed like he wanted to find somebody to blame for things.'

'Is there anything here on those investigations?'

'Maybe in his desk. Probably in the safe.'

'Guess we'll have to wait to get into the safe with a warrant, or cooperation from his lawyer. That would be Glen Caulkins. You wouldn't have the combination, would you?'

'Not very likely! He trusted me to get the paper printed, and on time, but that's about all.'

Charles had been opening desk drawers and pawing through the contents. Not finding anything of interest except some more real estate brochures, he said, 'These folders. We found some at his house, too. Had Edwards been buying any property that you know of?'

'Yeah, I heard he bought several parcels of land up north of here. Farmland, though I doubt he had farming in mind.'

'I wonder what he did have in mind. Maybe some sort of industry? He never did anything without a reason. Curiouser and curiouser,' said Charles.

'That's right, Alice.'

'Huh?'

'*Alice in Wonderland*. Your quote. Any more you want from me? I do still have a paper to get out, and we need a statement from you about this murder.'

'Say investigations are continuing and we expect an arrest soon.'

'Do you really?'

'No, but you can say so,' grinned Charles. 'You'll be among the first to know when we have something solid.'

'Guess I'll have to be satisfied with that. Nothing more you can tell me?'

'Not right now. We're only beginning to get a handle on things and we seem to have more questions than answers so far. Though I wouldn't want you to quote me on that. Call the station and I'll tell them to give you all the particulars, all we have that is printable.'

'Okay. Thanks, if that's all you can give me. By the way, we have someone coming in who might want to buy the paper, so we may be able to keep goin' and let the lawyers worry about the legal bits.'

Waving cheerfully, he plunged back into the hallway, calling to people as he went and gathering some of them into his office.

Charles closed the desk drawers and looked around the room. Like Jerome's den at his home, it was scrupulously neat. Not as much as a paper clip disturbed the austere orderliness. Pictures of Jerome with various dignitaries lined the walls. Jerome standing with the Governor of the state; Jerome shaking hands with the mayor; Jerome at some groundbreaking ceremony, leaning on a shovel. All around the walls they marched. Charles saluted the picture wall with a wry grin, wondering why there wasn't a picture of Jerome with the Pope. Even he couldn't swing that, I guess, he laughed.

And in the corner of the room stood a good-sized, sturdy-looking old-fashioned safe.

'That's probably where we should find some answers,' Charles said to himself. 'If only that safe could talk.'

He glanced once more around the room, then put on his hat and left the newspaper building.

The Bank of Sunbury sat on a downtown corner. A solid no-nonsense building that fairly shouted 'Trust me with your money!' Charles pushed through the front doors and nodded at the guard stationed there. He walked to the series of offices on his right, and stopped at the farthest one. There were no doors, only open doorways, and Charles could see that Mr. Sellers, the bank president, was alone at his desk. As he caught sight of the Captain approaching, Sellers stood and held out his hand.

'Good afternoon, Captain Charles. How can I help you?'

Charles shook the banker's hand and sat in one of the two chairs in front of the desk.

'Well now,' Charles began, 'I have a paper that says I can look in Jerome Edward's lock box.' Taking it out of an inside pocket, he handed the warrant to Sellers.

'Oh, yes,' Sellers said. 'That was a bad business. A bad business indeed.'

The bank president read through the warrant, then punched a button on his telephone, asking one of the employees to come to his office. In very short order, a young woman appeared. Giving her instructions and the key Charles had given him from Jerome Edward's key ring, he told her to bring the box to his office. After a short wait, during which the men made desultory conversation about the weather and the economy, the young employee returned and laid the box on Sellers's desk.

'I'm not sure that Mr. Edwards's attorney shouldn't be a part of this,' Sellers said uncertainly.

'I won't take anything away with me. You can be my witness to that. All I want is an accounting of the contents.'

'Very well,' the banker said, opening the box.

Together they lifted out the papers and other material and laid them in piles on the desk. Several deeds to properties which Charles detailed in his notebook; a great amount of cash, which they counted; a jeweler's box containing a diamond ring, and another holding a pair of diamond-studded cuff links; bonds, insurance papers and some stock certificates.

'Well, it seems to be the usual things we all keep in our safe deposit box,' Sellers said, 'Though not usually all that money.'

'Yes, that's a little odd,' Charles mused. 'Fifty-five thousand dollars is a lot of money to be keeping in a lock box. Wonder why he didn't just deposit it into his account. Unless he didn't want anyone to know he had it, or maybe because he needed to get to it in a hurry. Or maybe he didn't want it traced back to him. What other reasons do you suppose he would have for keeping all this money in here?'

'I'm sure I couldn't make a guess. I'm quite surprised to find it. Like you, I would have thought he would have put it in one of his accounts,' Sellers said.

'You wouldn't know when any of this was put in the box, would you?' Charles asked.

'There would be no way we could tell that. We have a record of each visit, of course, but not what went in or came out of the box. That's always a private thing for the bank's customers,' Sellers replied. 'I can get you the records of his visits, if you think that might help.'

'Okay. Do that. I don't know if it will tell us anything, but you never know what little piece of evidence will lead to a solution,' Charles said, while putting everything back in the safe deposit box.

'Thanks for your help. I'll leave this with you, and I'll see that Glen Caulkins gets the key that belonged to Jerome.'

He closed the lid of the box and again shook Sellers's hand.

As he made his way through the bank, he spotted Judge Laurence at the table in the center of the room, making out a deposit slip. He stopped beside him and said, 'Good afternoon, Judge. Oh, sorry, didn't mean to startle you,' as the judge gave a little jump and the pen skidded across the paper.

'Oh, Charles, you did startle me. Guess I was concentrating on what I was doing and I didn't see you come in,' the judge replied, putting away his fountain pen.

'Just checking on some things in here,' Charles said.

'Have you made any progress in your investigation into Jerome's death?' the old man asked.

'Some, yeah, some. We've made some steps, but it hasn't gotten us very far yet. I was going to talk to you…'

'Well, any help I can give you, Captain, I'd be very happy to impart, though I didn't really know Jerome all that well.'

'I only thought, since you are so close to the family, you might have some information that would help us find the killer. You surely would have known him, too, through some of the organizations you both belonged to.'

'I was acquainted with him, surely, but not to the extent that I would know any intimate details of his life. Of course, I would want to help in any possible way to bring this killer to justice.'

As he stood talking to Judge Laurence, Charles thought about the judge's life: lawyer, circuit court judge, then on to the Appellate Court. Now retired from active duty, he sat on several committees and still exerted a lot of influence in local affairs, as well as political matters in the state.

He was a good friend to Ethel Wagner, had been a close friend to her deceased husband. He didn't look his age. Charles had heard that he kept himself physically fit through weight lifting and swimming. Though he had to be at least eighty years old, he looked a healthy sixty-five. A full head of snow-white hair, growing low on his neck, reminded one of pictures of Clarence Darrow and his erect posture and well cut clothes gave an appearance of wealth, good health and authority.

Charles said, 'We're talking to all the people who knew or worked with Jerome. So I'd be interested in hearing anything you can tell us.'

'I will certainly give it some thought, Charles,' the judge replied. 'Have you talked to Paul Brady? He should know more about Jerome's activities.'

'I just came from there,' Charles said.

'Have you talked to Mark Kovich then? I saw Mark near the post office on Christmas Eve.'

'Are you sure?' Charles asked.

'Yes, I was on my way home and I saw him walking that way. I'm sure he didn't see me though.'

'That's interesting. Thank you, Judge. Come and talk to us if you think of anything else.'

'Oh, I surely will. Goodbye, Captain Charles.'

'And a good day to you, sir.' Charles sketched a salute and turned and left the bank.

Angles We Have Heard

December 26, P.M.

Perolli was waiting when Charles strolled into his office in late afternoon. The sun had come out and the wind dropped since the morning and now, though it was still very cold, it was almost balmy compared to the freezing cold he had encountered earlier in the day. Charles had enjoyed walking back from the newspaper office and the bank. Tossing his overcoat in the general direction of the coat rack in the corner, and rubbing his hands together he said, 'Lot better weather this afternoon, hey? Hope it stays awhile. Now, what have you learned?'

Perolli laid his notes and several report forms on Charles's desk and sat down while he read.

'Thank goodness I can read your writing. When I take notes even I can't decipher them. Okay. Mrs. Edwards. Says she was at home with her daughter. Not much we can do with that. But wait! Her daughter wasn't there when the patrolmen went to get Mrs. Edwards. And she hadn't been home either. Didn't they say she was driving in her driveway? Why would she say she was home when she knows we know better? Is that just arrogance, thinking we're not smart enough to put two and two together and come up with four? Wonder where she really was at the time. And is she lying because she has something to hide? Hmm.

'Well now, Mark Kovich says he was at the bar, like he told us earlier, but nobody remembers seeing him there. Course that doesn't mean he wasn't there, but when I ran into the old judge just now at the bank, he says he saw Mark near the post office later that day. More food for thought.

'Now, Stanford Bissell,' Charles said, opening another folder. 'Now this is interesting! His wife says Bissell went out about that time and was gone for about a half hour. Well, well. So Mr. Bissell lied to us. But could he have driven to the post office, killed Jerome and gotten back home all in only thirty minutes?' Charles chewed his lip and pondered.

'And does he still have a key to the post office, in spite of what he told us?

'Okay. Let's see what else we have here. Eric Ramsey claims he was shopping, and one clerk remembers seeing him in the store, but can't pinpoint the time. Well, it was Christmas Eve, always a madhouse in the stores. Mrs. Wagner was home alone, after giving her housekeeper the day off. Can't imagine why they even bothered to ask her questions. Certainly can't see her stabbing her nephew. That's one great lady. They even have the old judge here. Says he was home watching football on TV. Well, Perolli,' Charles said as he tossed the last paper on the desk, 'You and the boys have done a good job putting all this together. But it doesn't get us very far, does it? No one is completely out of the picture. And we have lots more people to talk to.'

Detective Robinson stuck his head in the doorway and said, 'We've been through the names in that address book of Edwards's and haven't come up with anything much.'

He walked to Charles's desk and handed him the book.

'Apparently none of these people could have been in Sunbury at the time of Jerome's death. A lot of them live out of town, some as far away as California. Most of these couldn't even remember who Jerome Edwards was, which makes sense. You can tell from the ink in the book that these names and addresses are pretty old. We have talked to most of them, but there are six or seven we haven't been able to locate yet.'

'Well, keep trying. I don't know if any of this is important, but we have to try all avenues. None of the people in here were in the neighborhood recently?'

'None we've found so far. Actually, several names in the book are people who have died, so at least we can be sure of crossing them off!'

'I wonder if it would help to run this by Mrs. Edwards. Maybe she would realized some of the names.'

'Couldn't hurt.'

'Okay. Do that, Robby. Let me know what you find out.'

After a moment, Charles said, 'One of our next moves should

be to talk to Glen Caulkins, Jerome's lawyer. I'm interested in seeing what is in Jerome's will and what is in the safe in his office at the newspaper. It's a little late to call now, better do that first thing in the morning. Remind me, Perolli.'

Charles pushed the papers on his desk into a pile, and said, 'Let's call it a day for now. About time we all went home.'

Charles wearily plodded up the walk to his front door, opened the door and called, 'I'm home, Marthie.'

He dropped his keys on the hall table and followed his nose into the kitchen where Martha was in the process of taking a pan of biscuits from the oven. He could also smell the delicious aroma of Martha's chicken pie.

'I'm so glad you're home,' Martha said, 'And just in time, too. These biscuits taste a lot better when they're hot. Get washed up and come to the table. Dinner is all ready.'

Charles gave her a peck on the cheek and went upstairs.

Later, having put away most of the chicken dish, several biscuits and a healthy helping of cherry pie, Charles leaned back in his chair, contentedly patting his stomach.

'Great meal, Marthie. Not all that good for my waistline, but it was worth it!'

Martha smiled at the compliment and said, 'Well, you could have left a little for tomorrow, but I'm glad you enjoyed it.'

'Tell me about this case you're working on,' she continued. 'It's a bad one, isn't it?'

'You bet it is. I can't seem to get a handle on it. There isn't any evidence to speak of. What I would give for an eyewitness or a fingerprint. Even one of those kooks who come in and confess to whatever crime is current.

'Nobody saw him, everybody who could be the murderer has an alibi of sorts, and Jerome was so secretive about his dealings that he hasn't left us anything to work on. What do you know about him? Any gossip you have come across?'

'Now, dear, are you implying that I gossip?' she said jokingly, rising and beginning to clear the table. Charles helped her stack the dishes and carry them to the sink.

'You know what I mean,' he said. 'In a town like this people talk. They talk about other people and it's a cold fact that Jerome gave them plenty to talk about.'

'Well, now,' Martha said, 'I have heard that he's been seen with a woman, a woman about half his age. No one seems to know who she is. Then there was his loud argument with a reporter who worked for him, right out in front of the bank. Last week, I think. And then…'

Charles began to laugh and put his arm around Martha.

'I'm sure glad you're not one to listen to gossip!'

Martha sniffed and said, 'All right, smarty. You asked and I told you. Anyone in town could tell you the same things. Jerome Edwards was so arrogant and so sure of himself, he did just what he pleased and thought he was God's gift to Sunbury.'

'You didn't like him much, did you?'

'No. He was not a likable man. Not that I had any personal dealings with him. Why don't you talk to some of the people he blasted in his newspaper editorials. If he wrote about me like that, I think I would have been tempted to go after him with a knife, or a baseball bat, or…'

'Whoa! I never realized how bloodthirsty you could be!'

Martha calmly ran water in the sink and added soap.

'All I'm saying is, people can only be pushed so far, then they begin to push back. And that man has done a lot of pushing.'

Charles picked up a dish towel and began drying the dishes as Martha stacked them in the drainer.

'You're right, honey, and it's a very good idea. I'll look into that in the morning.'

God Rest Ye Merry, Jerome

December 27, A.M.

In a police department, officers are seldom allowed the luxury of concentrating their efforts on only one crime. So it was with the Sunbury police. Other matters intruded and demanded attention. Charles sat with his co-workers, pushing aside the folders accumulating concerning the Edwards murder, to focus his attention on a house break-in, vandalism at the local school and a gas station robbery. He listened to reports of these crimes, asked questions about what had been discovered so far, and suggested procedures in each case.

The school vandalism appeared to be solved. Two young boys had been apprehended while trying to get rid of several spray paint cans, when the police arrived to question them. They had given themselves away in the first place when they trashed every locker in the school hallway, except for their own. Now it would be up to the Juvenile Court to decide what to do with the young offenders. Charles shook his head in disgust.

'What gets into these youngsters? They have everything they could want. This is a super good school, with all the latest computers and all that stuff. You'd think they would be grateful instead of hateful. Now the taxpayers will have to pay to replace all this.'

The house break-in and the gas station robbery had been reported the night before and seemed to be one of those hit-and-run crimes, with very little to go on. Hopefully, someone would come forward with evidence to point to one or more felons, but for the present, all they could do was the usual routine of questioning neighbors and customers, and going over what little they had found so far.

Hurrying through the paperwork, and dismissing the other policemen, Charles, dressed in dark clothes instead of his uniform, drove back home to collect his wife and then headed for the funeral home. As soon as Jerome Edwards's body had been released to the family, plans for burial were made. There was no reason to wait for out-of-town relatives to arrive. There were none. And what remained of his family seemed to want to get this over with quickly, and put it all behind them.

By 10:15, most of the members of Edwards's family had gathered at the funeral home, hoping to avoid the press of spectators. But, even this early, they had to thread their way through crowds of sensation seekers. Ethel couldn't help but feel that somewhere in that vast crowd, was the murderer of her nephew. There to gloat, perhaps? Or just to make sure Jerome was really dead and safely buried. She wondered how many of these people standing in line to enter the building, gathered in groups around the front and across the street, had been hurt in one way or another by Jerome. How many were celebrating, not commiserating. She shook her head to clear it of such thoughts, and, clinging to Judge Laurence's arm, made her way slowly up the steps, nodding to several acquaintances on the way.

Inside the mortuary, all of the seats appeared to be occupied, and the funeral director, Jonas Hughes, conducted them to the section set aside for the family. Ethel sat down next to Marjorie, squeezed her hand, and reached across her to pat Lydia's arm. Johnny Stevens and his wife, Vera, Jerome's sister, were seated on her left.

Five people, Ethel counted. Six, if she included Tom Laurence. All these others, or most of them, were here out of curiosity, not care or compassion. Not much of a commentary on one's passing.

She thought of the many times she had sat in this room, mourning friends and relatives. The worst of those times was when she sat in this very place for her husband's funeral. She couldn't remember much about that time. She had been existing in a daze, going through the motions, when others pushed or prodded her into chairs and through doorways, not really believing it could be true, that her dear Al was gone.

Other times, other faces. Even other undertakers. This would be the third generation of the Hughes family. Jonas Hughes III was today's custodian of the firm. He quietly stood next to her now, almost as a guard to protect her privacy, and that of the small group of relatives.

Ethel glanced around the room, spotting many people she knew. There was the housekeeper and her niece, Flora. Ethel had met them on the few occasions when she had been invited to dinners at Jerome's house, before the break-up of the marriage. In one row she recognized several ladies from Marjorie's circle of friends, and some clerks from John's store. She pulled her attention from surveying the crowd, as the minister stepped to the podium at the front of the room.

Charles and Martha arrived late and had to stand at the back of the crowded room, where some of those attending moved aside to make room for them. Charles's eyes roved over the room, much as Ethel's had, wondering if the murderer of Jerome was here. He half grinned to himself, thinking, Wouldn't it be something if one of these people would jump to their feet and suddenly shout 'I did it! I killed him! And I'm glad, glad, glad!' Martha noticed the grin and poked him in the ribs with her elbow and a little frown. He quickly smoothed his expression to a bland one and turned his attention to the minister as he began to speak.

The service was short. A prayer, a few verses of scripture and a hymn played by the organist. The minister, pastor of Vera and John's church, had not been acquainted with Jerome. Actually it had been many years since Jerome had set foot in any church, and in fact had been heard many times blasting any religious tenet and ridiculing those who believed, so the short sermon was a generic one. No bittersweet memories of the dear departed, no deathbed wishes recounted. And certainly no mention of the way in which Jerome met his death. Just 'ashes to ashes, dust to dust'.

Another hymn, and the Rev. Brown closed the service, announcing that it would be continued at the graveside.

The 'mourners' began to file sedately past the coffin and out the side door, some of them to follow the procession to the cemetery, others dispersing to their homes or businesses, or to a spot across the street where they could watch the main characters in this drama.

Ethel peered carefully at each person passing her. Was it you?

she thought. But facial expressions gave no clue. Eyes down, they slowly recessed.

The service at the graveyard was concluded quickly, and the family was relieved to be in out of the cold, gathering at Marjorie's home for a quick lunch. She had arranged for caterers to provide a buffet of salads, a varied selection of cold meats, and several kinds of breads and cheeses, and lots and lots of hot coffee to warm them after standing out in the cold of the windswept cemetery.

There was very little conversation. Marjorie said she thought the florist had done a nice job with the family's floral offering. Johnny remarked on the size of the crowd. Lydia wondered about a headstone, and they discussed this for a while. Probably not unexpectedly, Jerome was not mentioned, and as soon as was polite, they all made their excuses and left, back to jobs and homes. Marjorie left the caterers to their clean up and left also.

After attending the services at the funeral home, Charles grabbed a quick sandwich at home, and, changing his funereal suit for his uniform, he returned to the police station. Remembering Martha's suggestion about talking to the subjects of Jerome's editorials, he delegated one of the detectives to search through the newspapers and come up with a list of names of people Jerome had been particularly savage with. As always, thinking of these editorials, Charles marveled that Jerome had never been sued for printing some of them. Many of the writings had come dangerously close to libel. He wondered, too, how many people in town read and believed the invective.

Then Charles gathered together four of his officers and said to Perolli, 'Keep working on the names in the address book and the calendar. I'm going out to Edwards's house with this crew. When I get back, I want to go over to Rock Falls to see the people mentioned in Robinson's report.'

The policemen trooped out to their cars and drove to Jerome's house, where they were greeted by the housekeeper. After explaining to her just what they wanted, they divided up the rooms and began the search. Charles and another policeman, Andy Jensen, were conducting the search of Jerome's bedroom.

They entered a large room, at the front of the house, with floor-to-ceiling windows covered with dark-colored drapes. A king-sized bed, with carved headboard, was centered against one wall, with night stands on either side. A comfortable-looking armchair was in one corner, and one whole wall was filled with doors, behind which were clothes closets and cupboards of various sizes.

They began to open drawers and closets.

'Just look at this!' Andy said. 'All his underwear is in exact even piles. Looks like he measured the stacks with a ruler. And his socks are all folded just the same way, and even laid in rows according to color. Jeez, this was some neat freak! He'd drive me batty if I had to live with him!'

Andy continued to look through dresser drawers, while Charles tackled the closets. There too, neatness reigned. Every suit, and there were many, hung the same distance from the next one, and there again, they were lined up according to color, starting with gray, then shades of brown, followed by navy and black. At the back of the closet was a shoe rack, with ten or twelve pairs placed precisely.

Charles felt in the pockets of each suit jacket hanging in the closet and came up with exactly nothing.

'Strange,' Charles said. 'Not a note, a receipt or memo, not even a handkerchief – or even any lint! – in any of his pockets. Sure isn't like my coats!'

A shelf above held several boxes. Each of these was taken down and searched, the contents laid on the bed. They held hats, a plastic raincoat, and some boxes of what would seem to be gifts, opened but never used.

As Charles put the boxes back on the shelf and moved away from the hanging suits, he knocked into the shoe rack, and several shoes fell off onto the carpet. As he began putting them back on the rack – Gucci, hand-stitched loafers, golf shoes hardly worn, patent leather evening pumps, and a variety of other types of shoes – something fell out from the toe of one shoe.

'Hello! What have we here? This looks like an exposed roll of film.'

He held it up to Andy. 'Hidden like that I'd say it's got to be something important. What do you suppose it is? Better get it to the lab right away. Maybe it will gives us some answers.' He put the film in his pocket and resumed his searching.

Further searching failed to turn up anything else. All they proved in their scrutiny was that Jerome had been obsessively neat. Charles stood in the middle of the room and glanced around. They had felt under shelf linings, the linings of the dresser drawers and had even emptied all the drawers and checked their undersides. Andy had even gotten down on his hands and knees and peered under the bed. On the bedside table on one side was a lamp and a telephone, the mate to the lamp on the other table. A telephone directory was in one table drawer. Nothing else stood on tables or dressers. Only clothes were in the drawers and closets. There were no personal touches, no family pictures. Jerome was obviously not a sentimental person.

'I wouldn't have expected him to have a souvenir pillow saying "Welcome to Niagara Falls" or something like that, but doesn't it seem odd not to find keepsakes of any kind?'

'He had to have been a very cold fella,' Andy replied.

'If he hadn't been this neat, he might have left us some clues to help us nail his killer,' Charles grumped. 'I can understand his being neat, but sure as Hell we should have found some papers, some indication of what he had been working on. We've been through his desk here at the house, and his desk down at the newspaper office. He couldn't have carried every detail of his business in his head. Course, there's also that safe in his office downtown. Maybe that will give us some help.'

Charles gazed unseeingly at the closet door. Suddenly he snapped his fingers and said, 'His briefcase! I know what's missing, his briefcase! He had to have had one, but it sure isn't anywhere we've looked. Now it's possible he had it with him when he was killed and the murderer took it with him. Or her. But if not – what about his car? It could be there, too. It wasn't found at the post office. Gotta find out how the search for his car is coming.

'Well, guess there's not much more we can do here, Andy. Unless you can think of something we have overlooked.'

'No, can't think of a thing.'

'Okay. Let's see if the boys have had any better luck in the rest of the house.'

But the other policemen who had been searching the other rooms in this large mansion, had come up with the same result: zilch. They all agreed that they had never come across a neater, more orderly home, and the crew left shaking their heads in frustration. All of them had participated in police searches of one kind or another, from mighty palace-like houses to the poor, rundown, garbage-strewn hovels of the very poor, but never had they come up with so little information. Except for the roll of exposed film. All agreed that that could be the most illuminating clue so far, and perhaps the evidence that could solve the case. Perhaps the afternoon wasn't a total loss after all.

Deck Rock Falls With Boughs of Holly

December 27, P.M.

In the mid-afternoon, the sun had begun to shine on snow packed roads as Captain Charles and Perolli drove the eight miles to the little town of Rock Falls. This was the county seat, a bustling place in spite of its size, with Victorian architecture, gaslight-replica lamp posts and tree-lined streets.

Even in these days of glass and chrome, Rock Falls had resisted the trend toward modernization, and outwardly remained untouched by the twentieth century. There might be fax machines and air conditioners inside the buildings, but on the outside this town remained a nineteenth-century jewel, due to local ordinance's forbidding the construction of any building unless it conformed to the Victorian style. Any repairs or renewal of buildings also had to retain this influence. As a result, it was a unique and charming village, one by which all Rock Falls residents set great store.

Many of the private residences were three- and four-genera-tion homes. Although the city's laws concerning architecture did not apply to the residential areas, there were few homes that were less than forty or fifty years old. Two-storey dwellings, built in the days when families were large, often including elderly parents or orphaned cousins, with wrap-around verandahs, usually populated in the summer months by wicker rocking chairs were commonplace, as were roller-skating adolescents tearing up and down the shady sidewalks, though many of these teens and younger children had opted for the new fad of rollerblades. Visitors from afar might think they had walked into another era through a time warp. Rock Falls people were proud of their community and fought vigorously any attempt to modernize it. It was a gentle, sleepy little village, but it had kept pace with the rest of the world as far as commerce and industry were concerned. A book publisher was located here, its plant a copy of an eighteenth-century mansion.

There were several cottage industries, a computer programming service, an ice cream plant, and, of course, the legal fraternity concerned with court affairs, trials et al.

After reading the reports of the patrolmen who had been looking into Jerome Edwards's activities immediately prior to his death, Charles had become curious about the witnesses interviewed here in Rock Falls and wanted to talk to them first hand. Checking the address in the file on his lap, he pointed and Perolli pulled the car into a parking space in front of the hardware store.

'This should be it,' Charles said. 'Monroe's Hardware. Mr. Cedric Monroe is the man we want to talk to.'

They got out of the car and walked to the front of the store. It was decorated like the rest of the stores on the street, with small decorated trees in most windows, wreaths hanging from the lampposts and lights outlining doors and windows. Charles looked around at the Victorian decorations, and thought he would not be surprised to see a horse and sleigh coming down the street.

An old-fashioned bell attached to the top of the door jangled as they entered. It was a large, well stocked store, offering not only the traditional hardware items, such as nails and hoes and hammers, but also cookware and faucets of very modern design, and a multitude of other products. At the front of the store, a table loaded with merchandise enticed buyers with a large sign saying 'Christmas Lights! Half Price!'

Several customers were browsing in the wide aisles, and two salesmen were assisting others. Charles walked to the front counter and waited for the woman standing there to finish making her purchases. When the clerk turned to him, he asked for Mr. Monroe.

'Yes, sir. He'd be in his office. Just up those stairs,' he said, pointing to a staircase at the side of the front doors. Charles and Perolli made their way up and knocked on the door at the head of the stairs. Hearing 'Come!' they entered a charming, spacious room. It was a pleasant place in which to work, taking up most of the width of the store. Sunlight flooded in through the large window overlooking Main Street, and colorful braided rugs covered the wide boards of the floor. Mr. Monroe was sitting at a partner's desk, facing the window.

Charles introduced himself and Perolli, showing Monroe their badges. The store owner stood and shook hands with the officers, then bustled about, arranging lyre-back chairs near his desk, which added to the turn-of-the-century atmosphere, as though imitating, or attempting to imitate, the Victorian look of the exterior of the store.

Much of the wall space in the office was taken up with filing cabinets, but one whole wall was covered with framed oil paintings of lighthouses, harbor scenes and sunsets over rock-strewn beaches.

Monroe noticed Charles staring admiringly at the paintings and said proudly, 'My daughter's. She's studying art and I grab anything she will let me have. She's good, don't you think?'

Charles replied, 'I think she's very good. I wouldn't mind hanging any one of those in my living room.'

Monroe beamed in appreciation. He was a round man, his receding hair mostly white and cut long at the back, almost reaching his collar, and he wore what might be called a frock coat. Charles suddenly had the feeling he had stepped into a Dickens novel. Mr. Pickwick in the flesh! And the room extended the illusion.

'Well, sir,' Charles said, fastening his attention on the man seated now behind his desk, 'We don't want to keep you long from your work. Just a few questions we wanted to ask.'

'I'm not really surprised to see you,' Mr. Monroe said, 'After I talked to those other policemen. That's what this is about, right?'

'Yes, exactly. That's what we would like to talk to you about. Can you tell us any more about seeing Mr. Edwards here in town?' Charles asked.

'I think I told the other men about all I know. As you can see, when I sit here at my desk, I can see the whole block through that window. Kinda keeps me in touch with the town, you might say,' he said, smiling. 'Or maybe I'm just a busybody, wanting to keep in touch with everyone's business. You suppose?'

Charles smiled as he rose and went to the window, where he had a clear view of several blocks of Main Street in both directions. Seating himself again, he gestured for Monroe to continue.

'Well. I just happened to be looking out the window and I saw Mr. Edwards there on the street,' Monroe went on. 'I had seen him around and his picture had been in the newspapers quite a lot recently, so I recognized him right away. And then, when I heard he was dead, I mentioned it to some people. You know, like you say, "Why, I just saw him the other day, and now he's dead." Sorta like you're part of the news or something.'

'Yessir, I understand that. Now can you tell us just what you saw?'

'Well, like I said, I was looking out the window – gee, you fellows are going to think I do nothing else! Anyway, I was just kind of idly looking and I saw Mr. Edwards standing across the street by the sporting goods store. And these two men – Well, at first I thought they were threatening him.'

'What made you think that?'

'They were right up in his face, real menacing like, and one of them shook his fist at him. But then, they stepped back, and seemed to be laughing. So maybe I was wrong about the threat part.'

'Could you see where they went?'

'No. Just west on Main Street.'

'By any chance did you see a car they were driving?'

'Why, yes, didn't I say that? They got in a big black car – Caddy, I think – and took off down the street, west, like I said.'

'Did you notice the license number?'

'Why, no. I didn't even think of looking for it.'

'And Mr. Edwards? What did he do?'

'He stood there a while, just a few seconds, then kinda shook his head and walked on down the street.'

'And did you see where he went?'

'No. I went back to my work, and I wasn't looking out the window anymore.'

'What time of day would this have been?'

'Probably three, three thirty. Middle of the afternoon anyway. I remember I took my coffee break just afterwards. It was about this time of day.'

'And this was December 22, right?'

'Yes, that's right.'

'Could you describe the men who were talking to Edwards?'

'Oh, if I had to give a description, I'd say they looked like the movie idea of gangsters,' he laughed. 'You know, black raincoats, black snap-brim hats, couldn't see their faces. They weren't anyone I had seen in town before though, I'm pretty sure of that. And they *did* look a little scary. Sure didn't look like they belonged in Rock Falls.'

'Did you talk to anyone else about this?'

'Yes, I had lunch with George the next day, and I told him about it. That's George Adams, over at the Court House. And he said he had seen them, too.'

'Yes, we have his name on the report. I know George. We'll go talk to him.'

Standing, Charles again shook Monroe's hand and said, 'Thanks. Eyewitnesses like you are a big help to us.'

'Glad to help. I'll be curious to see how all this will come out.'

'So will we, Mr. Monroe, so will we. And tell your daughter to keep up the good work. We may see her paintings in an art museum some day.'

Mr. Monroe smiled widely and shook hands again with both policemen.

'I will certainly tell her that,' he said. 'These kids need all the encouragement they can get.'

Charles and Perolli made their way back down the stairs and out of the hardware store, then turned left on their way to the Court House a block away.

The Court House sat solidly in the center of the downtown commercial district, taking up an entire block. If the town was a little jewel, this building was its twenty-four carat gold setting. Its colonnaded porticos on all four sides gave the impression of a Victorian mansion, complete with multiple chimneys, turreted towers at each corner and gingerbread edging on the roof. It was three storeys high, painted a cream tint, with a dark red roof and matching trim around the windows. An American flag flew from the clock tower in the center of the roof, and around the building on all sides were grassy areas, benches, and, on two corners, memorials to distant wars. In honor of the Christmas season, the large tree on a third corner was decorated with multi-colored lights.

The two policemen climbed the steps and hesitated inside the doors as their eyes made the adjustment from bright sunlight reflecting off the snow to the dark interior of the old edifice. Wide, creaking floorboards showed evidence of a great many feet treading this way over the years. A wide center area was surrounded by stairs on two sides and doors identified by signs projecting from the tops of doorways: County Treasurer, Circuit Clerk, etc. As they headed for the County Clerk's office, they spied George Adams talking to two other men, all standing in front of Adams's office doorway. Seeing Charles, he excused himself and walked toward the policemen.

'Good to see you again, Captain, Sergeant. I'll just bet you're here to ask me about seeing Jerome Edwards here in town last week. As a matter of fact, that's what we were just talking about. The murder would seem to be the main topic of conversation here in town these days.'

'That's right, George. It's the same way over in our town. So, can you tell me anymore about this? How did you happen to see him? And where?'

'Well, now, I was on my way to the coffee shop, and I happened to notice these three men standing in front of Clint's store. You know, Clint has the sporting goods store, down the street a ways.'

Charles nodded.

'I was on the other side of the street, but I recognized Edwards, and as a matter of fact, I recognized the other two men, too.'

'You recognized them? Who were they?'

'They've been brought into Circuit Court two or three times on gambling charges. They don't live around here, but they have been involved in some illegal gambling, at least that's what they were charged with. But they got off each time with only a fine, though it's well known they were active in gambling both here and in the city. So I kinda wondered what they were doing here, talking to Edwards.'

'Gambling, huh? That's a new wrinkle. Never heard that

Edwards had any links to gambling.'

'Right! I guess that's why I was so curious when I saw him talking to them.'

'Could you see anything else? Hear any of their conversation?'

'No. I didn't stop, just went on my way. It was just that brief look. And I was too far away, on the other side of the street, to hear what they were saying. It was just a little odd, I thought; Edwards didn't seem to be the kind of person these fellows would be talking to.'

'You remember anything else that might help us?'

'Don't think so. I really didn't give it another thought until I heard he'd been murdered. Then Sid Monroe told me he had seen them, too, and we thought you might like to know.'

'Right, George. We've just come from the hardware store. If either of you should think of anything more, give us a call, will you?'

'Sure thing, Charles. What do you think about all of this? Have you any idea who the killer could be?'

'Nothing but a lot of speculation so far, George. Jerome was a man who kept things pretty much to himself. Didn't confide in anybody, so it's hard to know exactly what he was doing. If he had been more open, he might have left us some clues. And he certainly made enemies hand over fist. Didn't seem to make many mistakes, either, or none we've found yet, anyway. He just went on his own merry way, piling up money and property and political influence. Did you know him at all well?'

'Not really, no. I've been at the same meetings he had attended. And, of course, our paths crossed when he was running for District Attorney. Boy, that was a real smear campaign he ran! Maybe something from that campaign could be the motive for murder. Do you suppose? There was a lot of bitterness there. He ruined a few reputations and made a whole lot of people mad. But then, he lost. That should have been enough revenge for the people he stepped on. I can better see him getting killed if he had won!' George said, with a smile.

Charles nodded and said, 'Those are things we have to look into. We still have a lot of ground to cover. Well, take care, George. We'll be talking again.'

Frosty the Doorman

December 27, P.M.

As they walked back to where the car was parked, Charles said, 'The day Edwards was seen here in Rock Falls talking to those two men was the same day as the date in his calendar with the notation for dinner. I wonder if that appointment with the mysterious 'C' could have been here in town. V.C. could stand for Varsity Club. I don't know much about the place, but it's pretty exclusive and that would be the kind of place to appeal to Jerome. Might as well check there. It's over on Mulberry Street, I think.'

Perolli nodded, put the car in gear and drove a few blocks down the street, turning right when he reached Mulberry Street. He stopped before a white-pillared brick building, with a simple gold name plate screwed into the wall next to the front door. 'Members Only', it said.

'I guess if you're hoity-toity enough you don't have to put your name on the door. But this has to be the place. Let's go see how the other half lives,' Charles said, unbuckling his seat belt and opening the car door.

They climbed the short flight of steps covered with green outdoor carpeting, and entered the front door, where they were met by a stern-visaged man, in striped pants and black morning coat. Before he could object to their being there, Charles quickly fished out his badge and identification and asked to see the 'head honcho'.

'If you mean the manager, that would be Mr. Williams,' the man sniffed. He stood ramrod straight, as though there was a steel rod running down his back, and gave the impression of a palace guard standing at attention. Somehow he also managed to look down his nose at the two men, as at some lower species of insect.

'I will get him for you.' He gestured at an alcove next to the front door. 'Please be seated in the reception area.'

So saying, he marched down the foyer and quickly entered a room at the end.

Charles and Perolli moved across an expanse of plush, dark green carpet and sat gingerly in lighter green velvet armchairs, winking at each other. They looked through an archway at furnishings resembling a nineteenth-century gentlemen's club. Dark brown leather chairs, a deep pile rug in a pattern of several shades of brown, and part of a huge, stone fireplace could be seen. And above them hung a small, tastefully ornate crystal chandelier.

'You know what this place reminds me of, Perolli?' Charles said. 'That movie *Around the World in Eighty Days.* Ever see that? They had a place like this.'

Perolli smiled and nodded, looking around at the Victorian-like trappings, certainly at home in this unique town.

'How about this place, Perolli,' Charles whispered. 'Think we should apply for membership?'

Perolli smiled and shook his head, his finger to his lips.

A second man came striding purposefully toward them and introduced himself as Avery Williams, manager of the Varsity Club. He was dressed in gray flannels and a navy blazer, with what was probably the insignia of the club on the breast pocket. Tall, and extremely thin, he had the gaunt, starved look many fashion models strive for, with wavy gray hair combed straight back from a broad forehead. His attitude mirrored that of the first man they had met.

'What is it, gentlemen? What do you want with us?' he asked, with a haughty air.

Charles and Perolli stood and faced Mr. Williams. They introduced themselves, again displaying their badges.

'I'm Captain Charles from Sunbury, and this is Sergeant Perolli. We're investigating the death of Jerome Edwards. You may have heard about that. We'd like to ask you if he happened to be a member here.'

'Why, yes. He was. We were all devastated to hear of his death,' Williams said, but in a manner of one saying, 'Sorry your dog died.'

'Would he have been here for dinner on the twenty-second?'

Charles asked. 'You do serve dinner here, don't you?'

'Yes, of course, we do serve dinner here. But the twenty-second of December would have been impossible. Our dining room was closed all of that week, due to a small fire in the kitchen. Many special affairs had to be canceled or postponed because of it. It was most unfortunate happening when it did, just at this busy season.'

'I'm sure it must have been. Had you seen Mr. Edwards at all that week?'

'Actually, I don't believe I have seen the gentleman in question for quite some time. As I've said, he had a membership here, but to my knowledge, he has not been in for, I would guess, probably two months.'

'Okay. That's all we needed to know. Thanks,' Charles said.

The two policemen strolled to the front door, with Mr. Williams watching them all the way. At the door, Charles turned and waved at the manager. Williams did not respond.

As they sat in the police car, Charles punched Perolli's shoulder lightly and laughed. 'Did he think we were going to walk off with the silver or something? He sure kept his eyes on us. Maybe he just wanted to make sure we of the lower class didn't corrupt his high-toned atmosphere. That's some kind of place, isn't it!'

Both laughed as they drove back down Main Street. Then Perolli slowed the car and pointed to an awning extending over the sidewalk.

'Village Corner. V.C. Yeah, that could be it, too. Might as well check it out. Wonder how many more V.Cs we'll come across. Actually, V could be the person and the C could just as well stand for something else, like computers, contract, or something like that. And this could all be a wild goose chase, and the initials some sort of code that Jerome used for his own benefit. We didn't find any V.Cs in his address book, but it still could be someone he had just met. Anyway, as long as we're here, let's go in and see if this tells us anything.'

They entered the restaurant and walked through a deserted dining room, tables set in anticipation of diners with snowy white tablecloths, pale blue napkins folded into flower-like shapes and set in goblets at each place, and in the center of each table, a hurricane lamp holding a fat, blue candle. They skirted the tables and approached the bar at the far side of the room. One man, a large black man, wearing a black and white checked vest and red sleeve garters over a white shirt, stood behind the long bar, wiping glasses and storing them in the cupboard behind him. The bar was of antique oak, with a stained glass partition behind. It could easily have been transported from an English pub.

'You're too early for dinner, fellows, unless you want to make a reservation for tonight,' the bartender said.

Charles again displayed his badge and asked, 'Do most people make a reservation for lunch or dinner?'

'We don't do lunch, don't open until five in the afternoon. Yeah, they do make reservations if they want to get a table without waiting a coupla hours.'

'Who takes the reservations?' Charles asked.

'Our head waiter, Pete. He's in the back. Want me to get him for you?'

'Yes, we'd like to talk to him,' Charles answered.

The bartender walked along the bar, calling in a deep bass voice, 'Hey, Pete, some fuzz here to see you.'

Charles and Perolli grinned at each other.

A tall, thin man in maroon pants and checkered vest matching that of the bartender, hurried out of a door at the end of the bar, rolling down his sleeves as he came. He stopped before the policemen and said nervously, 'You men wanted to see me? Is there a problem?'

'We just want to ask you about a customer, or maybe a customer, of yours. Would you have the dinner reservation list for three days before Christmas?'

'Gosh, we don't save those. We just keep them for the evening and then throw them away.'

'Well, can you remember any of them? Do you remember if Jerome Edwards was here that night? That would be December 22.'

'Do I! He sure was! And he was a real pain! Didn't like the way his steak was cooked, complained that the potato was undercooked and even sent back his salad. Made a big fuss about it. Insisted on talking to the cook. And after all that, he left one penny for the tip! What a jerk! Don't know what his problem was, but he sure was out for blood.'

'Was he with anyone?' Charles asked.

'Yeah, he was with one of the secretaries from the Court House. I know her and I was surprised to see her with that idiot!' Pete replied.

'What's her name?'

'She's Cynthia Gibbs. I think she works for the District Attorney's Office.'

Charles looked at Perolli and said, 'Well, there's our C.'

'I hope I'm not saying anything that will get Cynthia in trouble,' Pete said, frowning, 'I know who she is because she comes in quite often with some of the women who work in the Court House. She's really a nice young lady.'

'You're sure it was the 22 of December when they were here?'

'Sure am. We had a big party to prepare for later that night, and I really didn't appreciate all the time it took to straighten out Mr. Edwards. And poor Hilda, who waited on him, took quite a while to calm down. She was ready to quit on the spot. Then, of course, when we read about him getting killed, we all talked about it. Can't say any of us really felt sorry about it, just kind of excited about having seen him just shortly before he got himself killed.'

'Can you think of anything else about that night? Was Mr. Edwards as usual? Was he afraid? Nervous?'

'Not that I was aware of. Just throwing his weight around. But that was usual behavior for him, I guess. Course, I didn't actually know him, so I can't be sure what he's like normally. I just know what I hear. He hardly ever came in here.'

'But he has been in here for dinner before that night.'

'Oh, yes. And, of course, he was pretty well known here in town, so everybody knew who he was.'

'Okay, thanks. We may need to talk to you again.'

'No problem, Captain. I'm usually here.'

Charles and Perolli left the restaurant and, standing on the sidewalk under the awning, Charles said, 'I'm going to have to bring Martha here for dinner sometime. Looks like a nice place.'

Shoving his hands in his pockets, he said, 'Okay, let's get back to the Court House and see what this Cynthia has to say.' But when they inquired about her at the D.A.'s office, they were told she hadn't been in for the past week.

On the drive back to Sunbury, Charles sat thinking aloud, 'Funny Jerome should have been seen talking to a couple of gamblers. At least out on the street like that. Makes you think they might have waylaid him. He's not exactly the kind of guy who would hold a public meeting with people he would probably call "undesirables". And if they *were* threatening him as Monroe seemed to think, that opens up a whole new can of worms, doesn't it! But why in the world would Jerome be getting mixed up with gamblers? Doesn't seem to be his style.

'And, you know, if that was the middle of the afternoon, where was he until dinner with this girl? Let's see if we can trace his movements for the rest of the afternoon. Someone over here must have seen him someplace. And we still haven't found anyone who can place him anywhere the day before he died, or the rest of the day on the 24. That could be very important.'

It Came Upon a Midnight

December 28, A.M.

Charles was sound asleep and dreaming he was fishing on a beautiful tropical island. He was sitting on the beach with a fishing pole in one hand and an exotic drink in the other. The fish kept jumping from the pole into the creel, and each time they did, a bell rang. As the basket made more and more noise, Charles struggled out of sleep to realize that the telephone was ringing.

'What the...' He peered at the clock on the bedside table and swore. 'Three o'clock. Damn!'

Rescuing the phone from the floor where he had knocked it, he barked, 'Yes!'

'Chief! Thank goodness I found you! This is Morgan, over at the *Reporter*!' an excited voice shouted.

In his sleep-fuddled state, it took a moment for Charles to remember who Morgan was. Oh, yes, night-watchman at the newspaper building.

'Yeah, Morgan. What's up?' Charles juggled the phone and half reclined on one elbow, knuckling sleep from his eyes.

'The office has been broken into!' Morgan stammered. 'I chased this man, but he got away! He must have gotten into the building when I was on my rounds. I heard him and shouted for him to stop, but he knocked me down and ran out!'

The night-watchman, an elderly man, was nearly in tears, and talking so fast that Charles had trouble following him.

'Okay, Morgan. Calm down. What do you think he wanted?'

'I don't know, Chief. He was in Mr. Edwards's office and I think he got the safe open.'

At that Charles shot out of bed and lurched to his feet.

'Damn! Damn! Stay put, Morgan. Don't touch anything, don't do anything. I'll be right there.'

'Sorry about this,' Charles said to his wife, as she reached up to turn on the light. 'Damn and blast! If I'd only been a little quicker talking to Caulkins.'

He was hurrying into clothes, shoving his feet into boots and heading for the door all at the same time. 'Keys... car keys,' he mumbled. He grabbed them off the table and flew out of the house. His wife turned out the light and went back to sleep. Having been married to a policeman so many years, she took these things in her stride. He'd tell her about it in good time.

It took Charles only a few minutes to get to the newspaper office. Slamming on the brakes, he slowed to a stop at the curb, with a loud squeal, jumped out and jogged into the building. Morgan was there to open the door for him.

'I haven't touched a thing, Chief,' he babbled, running and skipping to keep up with Charles's long strides. The building was quiet. *The Reporter* had been 'put to bed' for the day and this was a time of calm, though Charles felt the opposite of calm, hurrying down the hallway he had just recently been down. He burst into Jerome's office to find his worst fears confirmed. The safe he had noticed in the corner of the room stood wide open, and papers were strewn around it on the floor.

Charles slammed his fist into the wall. 'Damn! Why didn't I get to this sooner?'

He stomped over to the safe and peered inside. Several file folders and some papers clipped together sat on the shelves. There were file boxes, neatly labeled, ledgers and a small stack of old newspapers in the safe.

'Well, whoever it was, he didn't take everything. Looks like he wanted something specific. And he couldn't have had very much time to go through all this.'

Feeling calmer now, Charles looked up at Morgan, still hopping back and forth like a wounded chicken.

'I'm sorry, Morgan,' he said, 'I wasn't thinking. Are you okay? Do you want to see a doctor?'

'Oh, no, I'm all right. This fellow just knocked me down. He didn't really hurt me. But I feel awful about this. How am I going to face Mr. Brady? I'm supposed to keep things safe around here. This is the first time anything like this has ever happened.' He was wringing his hands and pacing nervously back and forth.

'I'm sure Paul will go easy on you. You can't be everywhere at once. And someone planned this carefully, to get in while you were elsewhere.'

Charles had more than a sneaking suspicion that the old man had been asleep but he wasn't going to add to his worries.

'Can you tell me what this man looked like, Morgan?'

'I really couldn't say. He was dressed in dark clothes, had on a hat, so I don't know what color his hair was, and he ran fast, so I'd say he was a fairly young man. But he went by me so fast, and I was so surprised to see him there, and then he knocked me down to the floor before I could see more. That's about all I can tell you.'

'What about size? Was he big, little, tall, fat?'

'I think he seemed tall, but then most people seem tall to me,' Morgan said, from his five foot three height.

'Did you hear anything when the safe was opened?'

'No, I didn't see or hear anything. I must have been on the other side of the building.'

'Didn't see anyone coming into the building?'

'No, Chief. Like I said, first I knew he was here was when I started down this hall and he ran past me and out of the building.'

'Okay, Morgan. Take some time, get yourself calmed down, then see if you can come up with any kind of description. You may be able to remember more when you think about it. Then tell the policemen when they get here. And you'd better call Mr. Brady and let him know what happened.'

'All right. I guess I better do that right away. I'll go in Mr. Brady's office and call from there.'

Charles used Jerome's telephone to call the station. He told them what had happened and asked for a crew to get here stat. He piled some of the contents of the safe and everything that had been dropped outside it and laid the stack on the desk. Surveying the safe and area around it, he could find nothing else out of the way, or any different than when he had been here only a few hours earlier. There was nothing left behind by the burglar that he could see – the burglar, who could also be the murderer of Jerome Edwards. It was too much of a coincidence that both incidents should occur within four days.

The police crew arrived and Charles left them in charge, making sure they would dust for fingerprints and collect any other evidence that might be found to connect someone to this break-in.

'Check the doors and see how he got in. Then make a list of everything that's left in the safe,' he told them. 'And then you'd better give all this to Paul Brady. He'll want to put it all someplace for safekeeping. And tell him that I have this,' he said, indicating a small sheaf of papers.

Taking these documents, clippings and envelopes with him, he returned to the station. There he sat at his desk and sorted through the items he had brought with him. His eyebrows rose upon reading one document, and he put it in an inside pocket. He sat back and thought about this paper and also about what should have been in the pile, but was apparently missing.

When the day shift patrolmen, detectives and secretaries arrived at the station house this fourth day after the murder, they found their chief already in his office, poring over papers and making jottings as he read. Soon, two detectives were summoned to his office, along with Sergeant Perolli. Perolli sat in the chair at the side of Charles's desk, and the detectives leaned against the door frame and the filing cabinets. After bringing them up to date on the early morning happenings, he indicated the pile of papers on his desk.

'This is what the burglar didn't take. So, maybe we can assume that his purpose was to take away one or more things that would be a danger to him, or to whoever hired him. I really can't see any of the people we've talked to so far having the know-how to break into a safe. So we must be talking about another person entirely. And we can also assume that he found what he was looking for, because he was on his way out when Morgan saw him. That means we need to find out what's missing. Now, we know some of the things Edwards was investigating, and it would seem logical to assume there would be something there on those investigations. If there was something else he was looking into, something Paul didn't know about, then well, we may never find out. Or if he was looking into something and kept it all secret, only in his head, then we're in trouble there. But, let's work with what we know.

'We need to know, too, if he kept a lot of cash in the safe. Maybe this is just a straight burglary. Someone taking advantage of Jerome's death to get a little richer. Don't know who might be able to answer that; probably Paul Brady would be the only one who would know. The way Edwards kept everything to himself, no one else would be close enough to him to know things like that.

'And then, maybe Paul would know if there was anything else important in the safe. Again, knowing our Mr. Edwards, that's highly unlikely. He didn't have any confidants, or close friends he might have confided in. Sure would make our job easier if he had.

'Now, Paul said Jerome was looking into the hospital fire. There's nothing here on that investigation. I looked through the rest of the stuff in the safe, and there was nothing there either. Nothing about it in his house. So, O'Reilly, you take that and find out all you can. See if you can follow Jerome's trail and find out what he came up with, if anything.'

'Right, Captain,' O'Reilly said. Pushing himself away from the door frame, he left the room.

'Okay. Next. There's nothing here that has anything to do with gambling. If those men who were seen talking to him in Rock Falls had something to do with this, or maybe had something on him, or even, if Jerome had something on them, well, there's nothing here. So we need to continue to look into that side of things.

'Now back to the investigations Jerome was into, according to Paul. Chambers, you check and see what information you can get on that bridge accident last year in Port Haven.'

'Sure, but that was investigated pretty thoroughly at the time,' Chambers said.

'Yeah, I know,' Charles replied. 'But Edwards had something or at least thought he had something there, and nothing about it showed up in the safe. Go over the reports from the Court House. See whoever was in charge, then talk to anyone else who might have some information. Especially if they had talked to Edwards recently.'

'Okay, Captain,' Chambers said, as he too left on his assignment.

'Perolli, you and I will go back to the newspaper office and see what we can learn there. Let's look into the fireworks accident. They will have back issues of the paper, I'm sure. I think the paper was called something else then, but they should still have copies there. There were some old newspapers in the safe, too. I need to ask Paul if they were important, or had anything to do with what Jerome was sticking his nose into. And of course, we need to talk to Paul anyway about all of this.

'Then Martha reminded me of something I should have thought of: all these editorials Jerome wrote. Did he hit a nerve somewhere? Did he make somebody so mad they'd resort to murder? While we're at the newspaper office, let's ask Paul about that. Oh, and on the way, we can stop at the post office. I finally got permission to open that mysterious door. Had to go through the federal courts, since the post office is a government building. A lot of dratted red tape! We'll pick up the locksmith on the way.'

As he was talking he was moving toward the door and shrugging into his heavy overcoat. Perolli joined him and they left the station.

Bring a Torch – or a Key

December 28, A.M.

When they entered the post office, they went directly to the Postmaster's office at the far left of the counter and knocked on the door. Several postal patrons were in the lobby, gathering mail from their boxes, and one woman was at the counter mailing a package. All eyes turned toward the policemen who were followed by Archie Black, the locksmith. Harold Duane opened his office door and greeted the group sourly, saying, 'Well, what is it this time, Captain?'

'Harold, we have a federal order here that says we can open that door at the other end of the lobby, and Archie here is going to do it for us.'

'Let me see the paper, Captain,' Duane said.

'Here you go, Harold,' said Charles, handing it to him.

'Hmm. Well, this seems to be in order. I'll go with you. I have to admit I'm curious about that door, now that it has been brought to my attention.'

The four men crossed the lobby and again all eyes followed them with curiosity. They stopped in front of the narrow door, and Archie took out a large assortment of keys. Examining the keyhole, he selected one key, then another, until he finally had the door unlocked. He pushed on the door, which at first refused to give. Another harder shove, and protesting hinges, apparently unused for many years, gave a loud shriek, and the door slowly opened. They heard a loud gasp from the customers in the lobby, and excited chatter. Many surged excitedly toward them.

The group around the door hesitated momentarily, then Charles moved forward and took two or three steps into the room, motioning the others back as he gazed around the area. It was a very small room, no larger than five feet wide by about eight feet long, and completely empty. Directly in front of this door was another door, seeming to lead outside, and what Charles was positive were blood stains on the floor. The outside door had a small keyhole, but no knob, only a push bar, which was probably why no one had ever suspected there was a door there.

'Looks like we've found the place where Edwards was killed,' Charles said, backing out of the doorway. 'Lock this door again Archie. Harold, I'll be sending a crew over here to examine the room thoroughly.'

'Yes, of course,' Harold said, looking pale and shocked.

They pulled the door shut, again with difficulty, and with loud grating noises. The locksmith locked the door and handed the key to Charles.

'You'll need this,' he said. 'You can get it back to me when you're through with it.'

'Thanks, Archie. I'll do that.'

A crowd had gathered in the post office lobby, as word had spread of this new development in the case. The case had the whole community excited and interested, and all were avid for news and every new development was greeted with ghoulish pleasure.

Waving his hands, Charles called, 'Okay, okay. Everyone just go on about their business. Nothing more to be seen here.'

He ignored the shouted questions and reaching hands, and he and Perolli and the locksmith left the building.

Do You See What I See?

December 28, A.M.

Paul was glad to see the two policemen, anxious about the robbery at his place of business, and eager for a good lead on an exclusive story for the next edition.

'Charles! You're just the man I need to see! What's going on? Have you found out anything about the break-in? Who do you think it could have been? And how in the world did he get in? Maybe more important, what did he want, or what did he get?' he asked, propelling the men back into his office.

Charles related everything he knew about the early morning event and their investigation so far, which didn't seem to be anything more than speculation, with few facts.

'We had a crew checking for fingerprints and any other evidence to be found at the scene. What do you know about what might have been in the safe?'

Paul Brady ran his fingers through already rumpled hair. 'Darned if I know. You know how Jerome operated. Didn't take me into his confidence. I would think it would just be newspaper business. Maybe the things he was working on. You know, the things I told you about. He was pretty secretive about all that. I would expect him to have put that sort of thing in the safe.'

'Any money or valuables in the safe?'

'Gee, I don't know. Somehow I doubt it, but how would I know? You know he didn't take me into his confidence! I still think it would just be newspaper stuff. Of course, if he had to pay for some information, I suppose he could have had money in there. But it wouldn't be well known; I mean, what robber would think this would be a place to get a lot of cash? There are certainly other places they would think of first.'

'Yeah, that's kinda what I thought, too. Now, we know some of the things he was looking into, those things you told me about.

But there was nothing in the safe that had anything to do with those investigations. At least, not now, if there ever was. As a long shot, we're checking into those matters. So,' Charles concluded, 'we'd like to look through the old issues of the newspaper. It was called something else back forty years ago, wasn't it?'

'Yes, it was the *Times Review* back then,' Paul said. 'But we have all that on microfilm. What issues do want to see?'

'The time of the fireworks factory accident. It would be sometime in June, late June, 1953. Maybe the 28 or 29; not long before the fourth of July, as I recall.'

'Okay. Come on downstairs. That's where our microfilm is. You should be glad we have it all on film. Just imagine leafing through all those old newspapers! Take you days and days! We'll get you started with June 1953. If there's anything else you need, just let Connie know.'

They had been walking down the stairs and entered a long, narrow room, lined with shelves on which sat tapes, boxed files and a varied assortment of ledgers. Desktop computers filled one side of the room and another wall contained eye-high filing cabinets in the usual sick-cream color. A young woman, Connie Travers, sat at one of the computers and turned to face the men as they entered the room. Paul introduced them and told Connie what was needed. She jumped to her feet and led them to a microfilm viewer, and after a few minutes returned with the film they wanted, placing it on the machine.

'Do you know how to work this?' she asked.

'I think so,' Charles replied. He sat in the chair in front of the viewer. Perolli pulled up another chair and leaned forward to read over Charles's shoulder.

'Just turn this knob and you can stop it anywhere you want, to read whatever you're interested in,' Connie said.

'Thanks. We'll be fine.'

'Stop back in my office when you're through here,' Paul said. 'I need to know more about what happened last night. I have a few more questions for you.'

'We'll do that,' Charles answered.

As Paul left the room and Connie went back to her work at the computer, Charles turned to the viewer and rapidly twirled the knob, slowing as he came to the end of the month of June.

'There we are. June 29. It was the headline story. Certainly not surprising.'

He read quickly through the article. It told of a sudden explosion that had rocked the outskirts of town and had been felt as far away as the center of Sunbury's business district, around four o'clock in the afternoon. Only after the fire fighters had brought the blaze under control had Al Wagner's body been found in the wreckage. Many theories had been advanced as to the cause of the fire, but nothing was proven. A follow-up story in the next day's issue reported that no foul play was suspected, and that careless use of matches was the probable cause. Smoke inhalation was said to be the cause of Al Wagner's death. No other evidence of wounds or illness had been found, according to the autopsy.

A day after that the obituary of Al Wagner was printed. He had been a well liked man, a good citizen, active in civic affairs, a decorated soldier in World War II, who left a widow, Mrs. Ethel Wagner, née Chatsworth, and one son, David, at home. The obituary noted his varied business enterprises and memberships in local clubs such as the Rotary and Lion's Club, his church affiliation and participation in state organizations.

Charles flipped back to the day before the fire, looking at other news of the day. An investigation had been started looking into the claims of fraud in the city clerk's office; a hit-and-run accident had killed a young boy; building had been started on a new shopping center west of town; a custody battle had been still unsettled; there was a birth announcement naming the mother, but no father, at which Charles pursed his lips and scowled; and a group of citizens had been protesting the firing of a popular teacher by the school board. There were other mundane items: a local political meeting, two weddings, the appointment of Tom Laurence to the Circuit Court bench, and on the two days before that, more of the same type of local news, including an amusing story about a small child and a skunk at a petting zoo. Must have been hard on the old judge, Charles thought, losing his best friend just when he should have been celebrating his victory.

Charles sat back, drumming his fingers on the table, trying to sort out what Jerome might have seen or heard. Otherwise, why would he have been reopening this long-dead affair? Charles called Connie to his side.

'Did Mr. Edwards ever come down here? Ever look at these files?' he asked.

'I've never seen him down here. At least he hasn't ever been here while I was at work,' she replied.

'Has anyone else asked for this microfilm?'

'No, sir. Not from me. And I'm almost always here on a work day.'

Charles thanked her for helping him, and he and Perolli retraced their steps back to Paul's office.

'Paul, just an idea – I asked the guys to gather some of the editorials Jerome wrote recently – that is, some of the more explosive ones. Maybe some of those that tore into some local citizen's reputation, enough to make them angry enough to go after him. Could you help us with that?'

'Sure I can, but I'm not sure I'll be looking for the right thing,' Paul answered slowly.

'Okay,' Charles said. 'How about if I send someone over here to check them?'

'That would be better. I'd hate to miss something that would really help you find the murderer. I might be looking for the wrong things.'

'Sure. I understand. You pull out all his recent editorials and we'll go through them. Mostly what we would be looking for is motive. Jerome could have, and probably did, ruin someone's reputation, or got them fired, or maybe messed up a marriage, like he did to his own daughter. And he could have, in all innocence, found out something that threatened somebody. I know it's all pretty misty, but it's one more lead to follow.'

'No problem. Send your men over and I'll have it all collected for you. Lord knows there was always enough dynamite in those editorials to push someone over the edge.'

'Thanks, Paul.'

'Now, about this break-in. What can you tell me?'

After giving Paul all the information they had so far, and answering his questions as well as he could, Charles and Perolli left the building.

'Did you come up with anything, any ideas at all, after looking at the microfilm?' Charles asked, as they walked back to the police car.

Perolli shook his head. Charles said, 'If there's more to this, something Jerome knew, it sure doesn't show up. He must have found whatever it was someplace else. And then again, maybe we're just chasing shadows.'

What Child is this?

December 28, A.M.

Charles and Perolli drove back to the station. As they entered, Detective Robinson stopped them, saying, 'We have the report on the fingerprints found on the safe at the newspaper office.'

'That was fast! What did they find?'

'The fingerprints belong to a known safecracker, Willie Best. Found the prints both on the safe and on the door he jimmied. Willie has a file as thick as *War and Peace* and has only been back on the street a few months. As a matter of fact, we were responsible for putting him in jail the last time.'

'I think I remember that. Didn't he get picked up on that bungled bank job?'

'Yeah, that's the one.'

'He's not too smart. Doesn't know enough to wear gloves. Must not read whodunits!' Charles grinned. 'Now why would he be breaking into the safe at the newspaper? It's not like he could expect a lot of money, or jewels or anything of the sort to be kept there. Lots of other places someone like Willie would think of first.'

'Got me, Chief.'

Captain Charles shook his head and continued to his office.

'Just like I said,' he muttered to himself. 'A screwy one.'

Perolli strolled into the office a short time later and laid another report on the Captain's desk. This one detailed Willie Best's most recent associates.

'Well, I'll be! So Willie has been palling around with that gambling crowd! Now ain't that somethin'! I knew this couldn't just be a coincidence.'

Charles read the report and then threw it in the basket with all the others accumulating since the murder.

'Now,' he said, 'just suppose Jerome has something that was a danger to these people. So they sent Willie to get it from Jerome's safe. Can't see Willie as the murderer, but his bosses wouldn't let a little mayhem get in their way. Wonder how Jerome was connected to those gamblers. Do you suppose he turned up something or other they didn't want known, maybe while he was looking into something else? Jerome would have been arrogant enough to try blackmailing them, threatening to publish what he found out in his newspaper, unless... unless what? Maybe money? There's that fifty-five thousand dollars that was in his safe deposit box. We still have no idea where that came from. That could be a dangerous business, going up against those people, and could certainly lead to murder. But then, if they paid him, why kill him? And what could he have on the gamblers that they would be anxious about? Have to be something illegal that could put them away. And if he had anything like that, where is it? Not in the office, not in his house, at least we've not found it so far.'

Charles sat, thinking, One more day with more facts, more people to see, more questions to ask, and fewer and fewer answers. Now this. Puts a whole new slant on things.

Detective Robinson stuck his head in the doorway and said, 'They've found Cynthia Gibbs. They're bringing her in now.'

'Who?'

'Cynthia. That girl who was having dinner with Edwards a day or so before he was killed.'

'Oh, yeah. Good. Good. Where was she?'

'She was lying low at her sister's. The guys asked around and found the sister was her only relative. So they went there to ask about her, just to see if the sister knew where she was, and bingo! There was Cynthia!'

'Good work. Bring her in when she gets here.'

Charles went back to poring over the reports. Why would a safecracker break into the safe at the newspaper office? Did it have anything to do with Jerome's murder, or was it just a fantastic coincidence? Charles didn't believe in coincidences. Certainly not in this instance. He wrote himself a note to try and find out exactly who Willie Best works for. Must be a police informer who would know.

And what about those investigations Jerome was conducting? Did they have anything to do with his death? Or was this something bigger? Blackmail, gambling, racketeers. More and more questions without answers.

A knock came at the door and Robinson came in holding the arm of a very pretty, very scared young girl. She was in her early twenties, with a cloud of auburn hair, and beautiful green eyes – eyes that looked fearful and desperate. Her short plaid coat looked more fashionable than warm and in fact she was shivering, either from the cold, or nerves, or both.

Robinson pulled a chair over in front of Charles's desk and gently urged the girl into it. She sat with her feet primly together, a black plastic purse on her lap, and her hands torturing a handkerchief into knots.

Charles put on his fatherly air and said, 'Now, you don't need to be afraid. We only want to ask you some questions. You aren't in any trouble.'

Cynthia stared at Charles and gulped, 'What... what do want to ask me?'

'We're investigating the death of Mr. Jerome Edwards, and we were told that you had seen him two days before he died.'

'Oh-h-h.' Cynthia started to cry. 'I knew something like this was going to happen. Something terrible!'

'Why is that?'

'He told me nobody would know.'

'No one would know what?'

'That I gave it to him.'

'Look, Miss. Maybe we'd better start again at the beginning. You're talking about Jerome Edwards?'

'Y-yes.' She mopped her eyes with the ruined handkerchief.

'All right. Where did you first meet Mr. Edwards?'

'He came to the office and asked me to do some work for him.'

'That would be the District Attorney's office?'

'Yes.'

'What do you do there?'

'I'm one of Mr. Emerson's secretaries.'

'Mr. Emerson, the District Attorney.'

'Yes.'

'All right. Now, what did Mr. Edwards want you to do?'

'Well, the first time, he just wanted some information about Mr. Emerson.'

'Mr. Emerson.'

Cynthia nodded. 'My boss. I thought he was doing a story for his newspaper. So I gave him what he asked for.'

'Which was?'

'Just some background. Actually things most everyone knows from the campaign.'

'Then he came to see you again?'

'Yes, and that time he wanted me to copy some records from the treasurer's office. I told him I couldn't do that, but he said if I didn't he would get me in a lot of trouble. He said he would tell Mr. Emerson that I had changed some testimony in the records to benefit some people who had been arrested. I didn't do that! Honest I didn't! But he said it would just be my word against his. I didn't know what to do!' she cried.

'So what did you do?'

'I finally got him the copies of everything he asked for.'

'When did all this happen?'

'He came to the office the first time about the middle of November. I remember it wasn't long after the election. That's why I thought he was only there to get some information for a newspaper article. I know he writes those editorials and I thought that's what it was for. I tried to tell him all the good things about Mr. Emerson, because I know how he can be really mean in his editorials.'

'And the second time?'

'About two, maybe three weeks ago.'

'And when did you give him these copies?'

'Just two days before he was killed!'

'When you had dinner with him at the Village Corner?'

'How did you know that?' Cynthia stared at Charles, her eyes wide and frightened.

'We heard. Why were you having dinner with him if he had been threatening you?'

'I had to. He said it would look more normal if I met him for dinner. I was afraid he'd keep asking me for things, but I went because I was afraid not to. I was so nervous, I couldn't eat a thing. And he was so rude to everybody. I just felt awful.'

Charles asked, 'Did you read the papers you copied for him?'

'No, he just told me which ones to copy.'

'So you don't know what they were about?'

'Well, I know they were payroll records and some contractor's bids. He just gave me numbers and dates.'

Charles had been making notes on a pad in front of him. Now he sat forward, his arms on the desk and said to Cynthia, 'You know that you are going to have to tell Mr. Emerson everything you have told me.'

'Oh, I couldn't! He'll fire me! Or maybe have me put in jail. Why did this have to happen?' She began to cry softly.

'I'm sure it won't be that bad,' Charles soothed. 'And it will be better if you tell him. We will have to know what was in those records Edwards wanted. He was obviously out for someone's scalp, and it just could be they were the ones who killed him. And then, maybe he really did uncover some graft or misuse of funds, something of that nature. Mr. Emerson surely should be made aware of that.'

Cynthia bowed her head and toyed with the purse on her lap, opening and closing the clasp with little clicks, her eyes beginning to fill again.

'Oh, I know you're right,' she said quietly. 'I guess I'm going to have to tell him everything. I should have told him in the first place. I just hope he will understand. I haven't been able to go to work the last few days, because I was so afraid they would find out what I did. Can I go now?'

Charles nodded. 'Your best bet is to tell Mr. Emerson the whole story. It will be a lot better coming from you and you know we have to tell him. Anything to do with Mr. Edwards's activities shortly before he was killed is important, and will have to be investigated.'

Cynthia gathered her purse and gloves and buttoned her coat, then left dejectedly. Charles said to Robinson, 'That gives us a few more names to add to our lists. And maybe more, who knows what goes on with that Courthouse crowd.'

After a pause, Charles continued, 'You know, Robby, the more we know about this man, the more I think of what his wife said. Out of a population of nine thousand, 8999 people would like to have seen him dead. Well, maybe not quite that many. Some of them are children. They may be the only group of people who haven't been hurt by this guy.'

'Oh, well,' he sighed. 'I guess we just keep slogging along.'

'I'll get going on the Courthouse deal,' Robinson said. 'Check back with you when I have something. ' He stood and left the office.

Ten Lords A-leaping...

December 28, P.M.

Charles and Perolli ate a quick lunch at the deli a block away from the police station. Anywhere they went now, people stopped them and asked for information about the murder. Some were merely curious, some frightened, others angry because the crime had not immediately been solved, and news of the investigation was scarce. This was a small town; everyone knew the Edwards family, or knew of them, and they expected prompt answers. Many had had dealings with Jerome, some happy, some unhappy, but in one way or another all had been touched by the man, directly or indirectly. And as Charles was well known, it was becoming more and more difficult to have lunch in peace!

When they had finished, they headed the police car down Main Street to the appliance store. Threading their way through aisles packed with stoves, refrigerators and freezers, they found the owner at the back of the store. John Stevens was a short, portly man of middle-age, tending toward baldness; he was dressed in brown slacks, tasseled loafers and a brown tweed jacket that strained the buttons across his middle. He grimaced at the two policemen approaching and said, 'I wondered when you would get around to grilling me.'

'Not exactly grilling, John,' Charles laughed. Charles and John Stevens had worked together on many community projects, had even coached rival little league baseball teams years ago. So it was with reluctance that Charles questioned his friend about his brother-in-law.

'You know I have to ask, John. Had you seen or talked to Jerome any time in the recent weeks?'

'No, I haven't seen him, not up close anyway. And you know how close I wanted to get to that vermin. I haven't talked to him in months. He didn't show up for Thanksgiving dinner, even though Vera asked him. She invited him without telling me first. Felt sorry for her poor brother all alone on a holiday. Believe me, we had words about that!'

'I can imagine.'

'I've been to a couple of meetings he was also attending, but we kept our distance. After what he did to me about that United Way fund, I could cheerfully choke him. And before you ask, Christmas Eve morning I left for Newark and didn't get back until almost midnight. And, I might add, three people went with me. I can give you their names.'

'Okay, John. Didn't want to leave you out,' joked Charles. 'But, seriously, have you any ideas? Anything you might have seen or heard? Any little hint about why Jerome was killed?'

'Not really. I have heard that Jerome was poking around into several things. I heard from people he annoyed along the way. Janie Thompson told me he was making waves over at the hospital. Trying to get hold of records that were not supposed to be open to the public. But, you know as well as I do, when that man got the bit in his teeth, he didn't let go! It's really amazing he didn't get himself killed years ago!'

'He wasn't universally loved, was he.'

'Ha!' snorted John. 'Can never understand how my wife and he can be related. She got all the good genes, I guess, and he got all the nasty ones.'

Charles laughed, clapped John on the shoulder, and left the store.

Back at the station, Charles and Perolli sat with file folders piled high, going over copious notes.

'There are just too many possibles,' Charles sighed. 'And we can't arrest a whole town. So many motives, so little evidence.

'So what do we have? The murder weapon was never found. The ME says probably a butcher knife. Could have come from anybody's kitchen. And we can't very well search every kitchen in Sunbury. Let's see that autopsy report again.'

Perolli reached under a stack of folders and handed one to Charles.

'Okay. Says here, the stab wound entered from the back, about midway down, and severed arteries leading to the heart. Just the one stab wound, no other injuries. The knife went through his overcoat and his suit coat and penetrated several inches into his back. That would indicate some strength behind the stabbing. And from the direction of the wound, the ME deduces the perpetrator to be of medium height – as though that tells us anything! And it was apparently a very long knife, since it went far into the body. Either a very strong person did this, or a very angry person. And a very sharp knife. Sure wish we could find that knife. It's probably been cleaned and put back in someone's kitchen drawer, or maybe thrown in the Sound and will never be recovered. Guess if I did that, I'd throw it away. Wouldn't want to carve the Sunday roast with it!

'Now, we're finding a lot of people who hated Edwards, and had a very good reason to kill him, but we already knew that. The sticking point, if you'll pardon the pun, is as I see it, not who wanted him dead, but how they did it. Okay, we found the little room in the post office and that has to be where he was killed. But who could have gotten in there? None of Edwards's keys would open either the door to that room, or to the post office, and I can't imagine why he would have a key to the building anyway, or what he was doing there in the first place. And there was nothing, nil, zilch, there at the scene. We checked the parking lot behind the building, but all the employees parked their cars there and everybody left from the back door on Christmas Eve, so the snow was pretty well churned up. Other cars coming later, Edwards or his murderer, or both, wouldn't leave any tracks to tell us anything.

'I still wonder if someone could have been in the building before it closed, hid in there until everyone was gone, then let Edwards in. I know what Duane has said, but it sure would have been hard to get into the post office after it was all locked up. If someone had stayed hidden until everyone was gone, it would have been easy for him to let Edwards in. Had to be someone with a key to that other door. Have we checked all of the postal workers? Anyone who was just hired maybe, for the Christmas season? Anybody at all who had a reason to kill him?'

Perolli shook his head and pulled another file out of the pile and handed it to Charles, who read it rapidly.

'Well, there's another good idea shot down. They all check out. Even the part-timers. Of course, there's still Duane. We will need to double-check his alibi. Have we checked on employees not currently working there, maybe fired recently?'

Perolli pointed to some lines at the end of the report Charles was holding.

'Yeah, I see. But, for crying out loud, if it doesn't have anything to do with the post office, then why in Hell was he murdered there, of all places!'

Charles paused and read another paper in front of him.

'They found Jerome's fingerprints on the door, that door that nobody seems to know anything about, and one whole palm print and some smudges. He and his killer must have shoved on the door to open it. We know how hard it was to open. And the blood on the floor matches Jerome's. It would have been a real shock if it didn't! We sure don't need another body, another mystery!'

Charles plucked another report from the stack leaning precariously on the corner of his desk.

'Now this leads us to believe that the break-in at *The Reporter* office was connected to gamblers. Same ones Jerome was seen talking to in Rock Falls, you suppose? And if so, what does it mean? Did he have something on them? Or did he have something they wanted to get back? Well, I guess that follows, they sure wanted something badly enough to get poor old Willie to break into the safe. But did he find it, that's the sixty-four dollar question. Then there's the young secretary from the D.A.'s office. We don't know yet just what Edwards had her copy for him. But if it implicated someone at the Courthouse in some unspecified crime, could be *they* were after some evidence in the safe. At any rate, Jerome's death scared somebody into breaking into the safe at the newspaper office, and making off with something, whether connected to the murder or not.

'And all that doesn't take into account all these investigations Jerome was tearing around town on. Did he find out something that was a great danger to someone? Or is it none of these things and just plain hate? Sure a lot of that around. Some person may have had it up to here with him, and let him have it.

'Then there's the money motive. You and I know that monetary gain is one of the strongest motives for murder, next to hate. Many many times it happens within a family. I have a call in to Glen Caulkins to check on Jerome's will and his financial standing. He's supposed to call me back. I would be very interested to see who inherits all Jerome's holdings. Should be a mighty good amount, from what we saw of his bank records, and all that money in his safe deposit box. That's still a very strange thing. Why should he have all that currency in the box?

'Then we still have that film we found in Jerome's house. Haven't found out yet how that figures in any of this.'

Charles stared off into space, his mind racing in all directions. So many motives, such a tangled skein of lives intertwined with Jerome's – but who could have hated or feared him this much?

He sighed, straightened up and said, 'Well, Perolli, might as well call it a day. Maybe something will happen overnight and it will all come clear. Sure could use a lucky break right now.'

He punched the file folders into some semblance of order as Perolli took his coat from the coat rack and started out the door.

As Perolli left the office, the telephone rang and Charles wearily reached for it.

Two Turtle Doves...

December 28, P.M.

Marjorie Edwards opened the door of her home as the doorbell chimed and held her hand out, saying, 'Eric, I am so glad you came. Lydia is in the living room. Come in, please.'

Holding his hand, she drew him into the foyer.

Eric nervously ran his other hand down the side of his trousers and said, 'How is she? Will she talk to me?'

Mrs. Edwards smiled at him and said, 'Yes, I feel sure she will. Come along.'

At the top of the steps leading down to the sunken living room, Eric paused and looked across the room to Lydia. His heart was beating so loudly he was sure it could be heard across the room. He went down the steps and halted a few paces from her.

'Honey, will you listen to what I have to say?' he asked.

'No, Eric,' Lydia said, smiling tremulously, 'You listen to me first.' Taking a deep breath, she continued, 'I've been very foolish, letting Daddy break us up. I should have had more faith in you.'

'Then you do believe me?'

Lydia nodded, tears in her eyes. In one long stride, Eric clasped Lydia in his arms, murmuring into her hair, 'Lydia, darling, you've made me so happy.'

Lydia's arms went around him and held him tightly.

'Don't ever leave me again,' Eric breathed. 'It's been so lonely without you.'

Lydia laughed breathlessly and whispered, 'Never again, darling.'

They stayed swaying in each other's arms until Marjorie's light cough parted them.

'Welcome back into the family, Eric,' she smiled. 'Although I never really thought of you as out of it.'

'Thank you, Mrs. Edwards.' Lydia and Eric grinned at each

other, arms tightly around each other's waist. The door chimes sounded again, and Marjorie went to answer the summons, saying, 'That will probably be Glen Caulkins. He called to say he would be coming to discuss your father's will.'

Opening the door, she greeted the lawyer, then frowned in annoyance at Captain Charles who followed him into the hallway.

'I hope you don't mind my coming along, Mrs. Edwards,' Charles said. 'When Glen told me he had an appointment here, I asked if I could tag along.'

Obviously annoyed, Mrs. Edwards said, 'If you must. I suppose it was inevitable.'

Charles grinned at the lawyer, shrugging his shoulders, as they followed Marjorie down the steps and found chairs in the living room. Lydia and Eric sat very close together on the sofa, hands clasped.

'Now, that's a sight I'm happy to see!' Mr. Caulkins said, smiling at the couple.

'Amen to that!' laughed Charles.

Lydia and Eric smiled happily at each other and tightened the grip of their hands.

'Glen, I am not sure why this visit is necessary,' Mrs. Edwards began. 'Neither Lydia nor I expect anything from Jerome's estate. He told me years ago that he was changing his will. He said if I did not come back and live with him as his wife, he would cut me out entirely.' She raised her chin and said defiantly, 'I made my choice then and I have not regretted it for one moment.'

'Yes, I'm aware of that,' Caulkins said, his eyes twinkling. 'But just bear with me for a moment. Shortly after your separation became definite, Jerome came to me to draft a new will. This left his assets, property and so forth, to the hospital. A wing was to be named for him.'

'Exactly,' Marjorie interrupted. 'So why...'

Caulkins held his hand up, palm forward. 'Just wait and listen please.' He continued, 'About two weeks ago, Jerome came to see me again about his will. For some reason, of which I'm not aware, he had become disenchanted with the hospital...'

'Oh-ho!' Charles blurted. Caulkins stopped and looked at him inquiringly.

'Sorry. Go on.'

'Well, as I said, he was not happy with the hospital, he didn't tell me why, but he told me to tear up the previous will that would have benefited the hospital. Right there in my office we destroyed his copy and mine. He told me he would get back to me with a new beneficiary. But he never did!' Caulkins finished triumphantly. 'Knowing all the people involved and knowing all the circumstances, I would call that poetic justice. You see, Marjorie, since he never did make another will, the original will, made shortly after you were married, and leaving everything to you, is the valid will. That one is still on record.'

He sat back in the chair, smiling widely. Marjorie, a stunned look on her face, said haltingly, 'Then the money, the house, the real estate...'

'And the newspaper, are all yours. Yes.'

Charles looked across the room at Mrs. Edwards and thought, 'Unless she's a great actress, this had to be a surprise to her. There goes her motive for killing Jerome.'

Glen stood and said to Marjorie, 'Now don't worry about a thing. It will all be taken care of. Make an appointment with my office for some time next week and we'll get things started for probate.'

She stood also and murmured, 'Thank you, Glen.'

Charles stepped forward and offered his hand. 'Congratulations, Mrs. Edwards. This should help to put things right.'

'Thank you, er, Captain,' she said softly.

The men recovered their coats and let themselves out of the house. Charles looked back from the doorway and grinned as he saw all three people in a group hug.

Charles and Glen shook hands and parted at the end of the front walk. Both drove off down the street, Charles deep in thought and not looking forward to this next interview. Minutes later he pulled the car to the curb in front of Stanford Bissell's house. He sat in the car for a few moments, with his hands on the steering wheel. Then, with a great sigh, reluctantly he got out of the car and walked up the ramp to the front door. Bissell answered his knock and invited him into his office, an area blocked off from the rest of the house, to create privacy for his business and also so that Mrs. Bissell wouldn't be disturbed by clients consulting her husband. The two men sat on straight chairs, facing each other. Charles reached into an inside pocket and pulled out a paper which he handed to Stanford.

'Yes,' Bissell whispered. 'I wondered if this would surface, now that Edwards's dealings are being investigated.'

He slumped over in the chair, the paper held tightly between his fists. Charles felt pity for the man sitting across from him.

'Want to tell me about it?' he asked quietly.

'Not much to tell. You've seen for yourself. It's a copy of a marriage license. I was married when I was eighteen. It didn't last long. Cheryl – that was her name – well, she left after only two months. I wasn't exciting enough for her. I never heard from her or about her after that. Most of the time, I just forgot it ever happened. That was in Ohio, and when I came East I met Margaret and we got married. Then, somehow, that devil Jerome found this marriage license. I have no idea how he could have heard about it, or knew of its existence. He wouldn't tell me. When he came to my office I thought he was here to get his taxes done.' He laughed bitterly. 'What he wanted was money. He told me if I paid him five thousand dollars every month, he'd keep my secret. Otherwise he would print the news as an interesting item in his newspaper, that I was a bigamist. I couldn't let that happen. It would kill Margaret. And she's been through so much already. I pleaded with him, but it did no good. So I sold some property I owned and I paid him. And there was no end in sight. He would keep me coming back to pay him more and more.'

Charles said, 'The night he was murdered, you said you were at home, but your wife told the policemen who came to talk to her, that you had left the house about the time he was killed.'

'Yes, she told me they were here asking questions. Actually I was taking a walk.'

'In all that snow?' Charles asked dubiously.

'Yes. I had to get out. I had to think. I was about at the end of my resources and I didn't know what to do. I was sure Edwards would never let this go, and I just couldn't find a way out. But that's all I did. I walked. I knew it would sound suspicious if I told you that, so I told you I was here at home. And I was most of the time. But I walked and walked, didn't even feel the cold. I was so worried. But then I came back home, with nothing resolved.'

Bissell hung his head, wiping his hand over his eyes.

'It would seem you couldn't have been the person who had the safe broken into, because you wouldn't have left this,' Charles said, indicating the paper Bissell held crushed in his hands, 'unless this is a very clever double switch. You might want us to think that way.'

'I'm not that clever, Captain. Tell me, how many other people know about this?' he asked, tapping the paper.

'No one. That's why I came alone tonight. You can keep that. But you know you will have to do something about your situation, and make everything legal. After all this time, a divorce or annulment shouldn't be hard to obtain.'

'Yes, you're right. Thank you.' Tears came to his eyes as he gripped Charles's hand in both of his. 'This has been such a horrible strain. But believe me, Captain. I did not kill Jerome.'

Charles put a hand on Bissell's shoulder as he stood and walked to the door. Stanford remained slumped in his chair, staring at the paper he held. Charles let himself out, closing the door quietly behind him. He walked back down the ramp and sat for a moment in the car, thinking, The robbery at the newspaper office had to be somebody looking for other evidence, and Bissell could still be the murderer. He certainly had good reason to kill Edwards. The break-in and the murder wouldn't necessarily have to be connected to the same person.

With a deep sigh, he started the car and turned toward home.

...And a Partridge in a Pear Tree

December 29, A.M.

As Charles began another day of collecting evidence in this murder case, a tall, distinguished-looking gentleman was ushered into his office. Wearing a black cashmere overcoat and carrying a gray homburg, he looked totally out of place in this dusty, untidy office. Charles looked up from studying the latest report and said, 'Yes, sir. Is there something I can do for you?'

The visitor replied, 'Captain, it's possible that I can do something to help *you*.'

Tossing his pen on the desk and sitting back in his chair, Charles stared at the man, wondering what this might have to do with the problem at hand. Or was he going to be given further problems?

'My name is Sheldon Jennings,' the visitor said. 'I have a law practice in Rock Falls. After hearing about the death of Jerome Edwards, I thought I had better come and talk to you. May I sit down?'

Charles leaned forward, his attention centered on this handsome, well groomed stranger. He took in the expensive cut of the man's suit and the scent of his aftershave lotion which fought with the stale smells of the station house. Yesterday's cigarette smoke and the overflowing ashtrays, and the greasy smell of take-out hamburgers, French fries and cold coffee almost overwhelmed the pleasant scent of Canoe. Charles recognized the scent, remembering the large bottle of the same aftershave still in his medicine cabinet at home, a gift from last year's Christmas.

'Of course, please,' he said, indicating the chair near the desk. 'Just what is your connection with Mr. Edwards?'

Sheldon laid his hat on the desk, sat down and crossed his knees, carefully smoothing the knife-like creases in his gray trousers.

'Captain, Mr. Edwards came to see me about a week ago to get my advice on a legal matter. I had never met the man before that time. Since this might possibly have something to do with his murder, I thought it best to bring it to you.'

'Interesting. Where is your practice?'

'In Rock Falls. Jennings, Keeler and Ellsworth. We're on Locust Street.'

'Now what kind of advice was he looking for?'

'He had what he thought was evidence that his chauffeur was a thief.'

'Buck Riley?' Charles asked with raised eyebrows.

'Yes, that was the name. The evidence was only circumstantial. Mr. Edwards wanted my opinion on whether or not there was enough to bring him into court.'

'What kind of thievery? What did he think he had been stealing?'

'Some valuable jewelry was missing. He, Mr. Edwards that is, had left two jeweler's boxes, one with a diamond ring and the other with some diamond cuff links, in his car. He had intended, he said, to take them to the jeweler's for repair. When he returned to the car they were gone. He said Buck Riley was the only person who had been near the car, so it had to be him. Before he went to the authorities, he wanted to be sure of the legal grounds, before he had him arrested.'

'And what did you tell him?'

'I told him he would need more proof than that before he could charge the chauffeur with robbery. He didn't have the car in his sight while he was gone, and he had no proof at all that the man stole anything.'

'I'm sure that was the right answer. We would need a lot more evidence to charge Buck with the crime. Where was the car parked when all this was happening?'

'That's just it. It was parked on Center Street in Port Haven. That's the main thoroughfare as you know, and there would be a lot of traffic on the road and many pedestrians on the sidewalks. It's a very busy place, and Buck Riley, also according to Mr. Edwards, spent most of the time in a coffee shop while Mr. Edwards was out of the car. Actually, almost anyone could have taken the jewelry.'

'And how did he react to your advice?'

Jennings smiled crookedly. 'Let's just say he was not a happy camper. But that was my advice, and I couldn't tell him otherwise.'

'Did he say if he had faced Buck with stealing these things?'

'Oh, yes. He apparently jumped the man right away. But Buck denied having taken the items. Of course, this is all Mr. Edwards's say so.'

'Well,' said Charles, leaning back in his swivel chair. 'I certainly thank you for bringing this to my attention. I'm not sure what it all means, but it does fill in a few holes. By the way, when was it he came to see you?'

'I looked up the date before I left the office. It was December 22. His appointment was for 4:00 in the afternoon, and as I recall he was very prompt.'

Charles wrote the date and time on a pad in front of him. Then, standing, he held out his hand to Jennings, who also stood and shook Charles's hand.

'Thank you for coming in. We appreciate your help.'

'Glad to be of assistance, Captain. If there's anything more you want from me, you can find me here,' the lawyer said, handing Charles his card.

As Jennings left the office, Perolli came in. Charles filled the Sergeant in on this latest development.

'It answers one question, about what Edwards was doing in Rock Falls that day. But it leaves us with even more questions. Buck told us Edwards had been hassling him lately, but he sure didn't mention this when we talked to him. He certainly didn't tell us his employer had accused him of stealing. Why? Unless he really did steal the jewelry and hoped with Edwards dead, no one would ever find out? And, of course, that would be a good motive for Buck to kill him, if he was afraid he would be arrested and jailed. Guess we'll have to go talk to him again.'

Charles had been writing all this information in a file and now he threw the file folder on the desk in frustration. It lay among a welter of files and papers. Charles stirred the mess with a large hand.

'Papers! Files! Reports! I tell you, Perolli, one day we'll all be buried in paper! Makes me feel like throwing the whole mess out the window.'

Then he grinned sheepishly. 'But then, I'd wind up being arrested by my own people for littering.'

At that moment, one of the secretaries came in carrying a large manila envelope and laid it on Charles's desk.

She said, 'Here are the pictures the lab developed from the film you found in Mr. Edwards's house. They said you wanted them as quickly as possible.'

'Great! That was fast work. Thanks.'

Charles took the photographs out of the envelope, shoved aside the papers on his desk and began to leaf through them.

As he picked up the first one he said, 'Good Lord! Do you see who this is? It's Vincent Fiorelli, the racketeer! At least we know he's a racketeer, even though we haven't been able to pin anything on him yet. And who's this other man? Can't quite make him out. Not in this one either.'

He continued to turn over the pictures.

'What in the world was Edwards doing with pictures of these guys?

'Hey! Look at this! Good God Almighty! Do you realized this fellow? It's Henry Tissere, coach of the hockey team. And they look very friendly.'

Picking up another photograph, Charles shouted, 'Now this all makes a little more sense. You know what we have here? These are photos of betting slips and odds. I'm sure this is proof that Henry was throwing games, shaving points to benefit the gamblers. This stuff is dynamite! If the gamblers knew Edwards had all this, it's no wonder they were all over him in Rock Falls.'

He handed the pile of photographs to Perolli, who stacked them neatly and put them back in the envelope.

'Where do you suppose Jerome got these? I can't see him hiding behind a dumpster or somewhere to take the pictures, but I sure can see him paying someone to do the job. And whoever took these certainly isn't going to come forward. He'd expect the same fate if he admitted taking them.

'Wow! This puts a whole new slant on the murder, doesn't it?

Now, if the break-in at the newspaper office was for the purpose of retrieving these photographs, they'll still be looking for them. We'd better keep a good watch on *The Reporter* office and Jerome's home, in case they make another try. Though the stuff in the safe didn't look disturbed too much. I was sure when Willie broke in he got what he wanted and left. If there was anything else in there...'

He pointed to the envelope Perolli was holding. 'Put those someplace safe until we can turn them over to the D.A. And now, let's you and me go see what Buck Riley has to say about this latest bit of news.'

But before they could start for the Edwards home, Robinson came in with an air of excitement, waving some report forms.

'Mark Kovich wasn't entirely truthful with us the other day,' he said. 'He *has* seen Jerome recently, contrary to what he told you. Not only that, but just last week, Mr. Kovich bought himself a gun. Got that from a pawnshop, when we were looking into those house burglaries.'

'What?' Charles sank back down in his desk chair. 'Now this is a surprising development. Go on. What else do you have?'

Robinson said, 'The bartender of a scroungy gin mill in Mansfield came in to tell us that Jerome and Mark got into a shouting match at his place over a week ago. He wasn't sure of the exact day, but he was sure about who the shouters were. Said they calmed down when he threatened to have them thrown out, and Mark stomped off and left. He heard his car go screeching away out of the parking lot.'

Charles grabbed the report and scanned it with great interest.

'Well, now, isn't this interesting! But it raises more than a few questions. What were they arguing about and why did Mark swear he hadn't seen or talked to Jerome in some time? What did he say? Three years since he had talked to him?

'And then there's this really big question... what in the world would Jerome be doing in a sleazy joint like that? It's hardly his kind of place.

'And, then, I know Jerome wasn't killed with a gun, but it sure is fishy, finding that Mark went out and bought a gun apparently right after this loud argument. Maybe he meant to shoot him, but another opportunity came along and he stabbed him instead. All of it does look very suspicious. We're going to have to talk to Mark again, that's for sure. But first, see if you can find out more about this big argument. Talk to the bartender, Robby, and see if you can find any of the drinkers who were there at the time. Maybe somebody will remember what the fight was about.'

'Okay, I'll take Chambers with me. What was the name of that place again?'

Charles glanced at the report and answered, 'Says the Green Parrot. It's down by the bay, I think. Go see the owner of the pawnshop again, too. See if he remembers anything Mark might have said when he bought the gun, or what his mood was. Anything else that might help.'

'Will do.' Robinson picked up the report and was on his way.

'Perolli, this man is one complicated individual. I would always think of him as associating with the elite. The "important" people.' Here he gestured ditto marks. 'The movers and doers. And here we find him in a dirty, rundown third or fourth rate bar, and talking to gamblers, maybe into blackmail, hiding pictures of racketeers. I swear this is one complex person!'

'Well, we still have to go talk to Buck Riley. Let's get goin' before someone else comes in and throws us another curve.'

Dashing Through the Snow

December 29, A.M.

As the police car turned into the circular driveway in front of the Edwards mansion, Charles and Perolli spotted Buck Riley walking toward the garage with a pail in one hand and cleaning materials in the other. He turned toward them when he heard the car approaching and stood waiting until they drove up to where he was standing.

'Something else I can help you with?' Buck asked, as the men got out of the car and walked to him. Charles was again impressed with the strength of the man.

'Maybe, Buck,' Charles answered. 'How about if we go in the garage to talk. Still mighty frigid out here.'

Buck shrugged his shoulders and led the way to the garage, a short distance from the house. It was a large building, holding three vehicles: a Mercedes, a Cadillac and a van. Gazing at these cars, Charles suddenly blurted, 'Are these the only cars Edwards owned?'

'Yeah,' Buck answered. 'He drives – drove – the Mercedes and I drove the Caddy when he wanted me to do the driving. The van is for us to use, Mrs. Worthington and me; we use it to run errands, grocery shopping and stuff like that.'

'Then how did Edwards get to the post office the night he was killed?'

'He must have driven himself in the Mercedes. I picked it up from the street and brought it back.'

'What? When was that?'

'Christmas Day. I saw it when I went uptown for a newspaper.'

'Where was it?'

'It was around the corner from the post office, on Elm Street. I'm responsible for these cars, so I brought it back and put it where it belonged.'

'Did you let anyone at the police office know you had found it?'

'No.'

'It should have been left there, Buck. Or at least you should have let some of us know.'

'Sorry,' Buck said, not looking at all sorry.

Charles seethed with frustration. How could they have missed this!

'Did you notice anything out of the way, anything unusual when you drove the car back here?'

'No, it was just sitting in the street, where he must have parked it.'

'Was it locked?'

'Sure, he always locked it, even when he was going to be right back. But I have keys to all of the cars.'

Charles shook his head in disgust. He opened the car door carefully and examined the interior without touching more than the door handle, then asked Buck to open the trunk. The trunk was found to be completely empty and everywhere they looked the car seemed spotless.

'Have you cleaned the car since you brought it back?' Charles asked.

'No, I was just going to do that now.'

'Well, just leave it alone and I will send someone out here to give it a good going over. We don't know that he was alone in this car. His murderer might have been with him, and his fingerprints could be in there. And there just might be something else that could help us understand how and why this happened.'

Charles turned his attention away from the car now and said to Buck, 'This isn't why we came out here to talk to you. We need to ask you... what do you know about some missing jewelry?'

'Jewelry?' Buck looked mystified. 'What should I know about that? What jewelry?'

'Some belonging to Mr. Edwards. We've heard he left some in the car, and came back to find it missing.'

'First I heard of it. Why should he leave something valuable in the car? That's not something he would do. He was always very careful of any of his possessions. And he didn't trust anyone. Even made me lock the car whenever he left it. When was this supposed to have happened?'

Charles told Buck what the lawyer had told him.

'Me? He accused me?' Buck exploded. 'I never took one thing of his! Never! What would I want with diamond cuff links anyway?'

Charles backed away and wiggled his hands toward Buck, saying, 'Okay, Okay. You never heard of this? Mr. Edwards didn't ask you about the missing items?'

'Hell, no. It's the first I heard of it. Not that Mr. Edwards would have shared this with me. In fact, he would have been all over me if he thought I had something to do with the stuff being stolen.'

'And he never said anything at all to you about it?'

'No. Not a word.'

'Okay, Buck. That's all we needed to ask you. And, Buck, if you think of anything concerning the car Edwards was driving that night, let us know.'

They left Buck fuming, hands clenched in ham-like fists. They got back in the car and drove back to the police station.

Charles charged into the station house in a black mood, what Perolli liked to call his 'heads will roll' mood.

'I want whoever is in charge of the search for Edwards's car in here now!' he shouted.

He stomped into his office and threw his hat and gloves on the desk, to add to the untidy pile already there.

O'Reilly stepped hesitantly in the doorway. 'You wanted to see me, Captain?' he asked.

'Were you looking for Jerome Edwards's car?'

'Yeah. Haven't been able to find it so far. We have a bulletin out to the state police. So far no luck.'

'Did it ever occur to you to look in his garage?' Charles snarled sarcastically.

'Well, sure. We looked there,' O'Reilly said in surprise. 'Soon after we found the body. Christmas Eve. It wasn't there, and no one seemed to know anything about it.'

Charles gave a great sigh and collapsed in his desk chair.

'And all the time it was just around the corner. Okay, O'Reilly, that's all.'

O'Reilly, looking a bit bewildered left the room.

'This is a fine mess. After checking the parking lot that night, we pretty much decided he either came with his murderer, or the killer took the car with him. Now this changes the way we've been thinking. There had to have been two cars. He met his killer there, at least it would seem he expected to meet someone there, whether the killer or someone else. He wouldn't just be wandering into the post office. And there was no way we could find tracks of another car, with the parking lot all churned up with the employees' cars coming and going, and snow on top of that.

'Now there's this thing with Buck. He could have brought the car back to the house like he said, or he could have brought Edwards to the post office and killed him. Which makes no sense at all. Why bring him to town to kill him if he wanted him dead? He could do that anywhere. And then, if he drove him, he always used the Cadillac, Edwards was the one who drove the Mercedes. But then again, it's just Buck's word about all the rest, too.

'Now this jewelry theft. If Buck knew Jerome was accusing him...' Charles paused, his hand in midair. 'Wait a minute! Where's that list?' Pawing through papers, he pounced on one and swiftly read it.

'There! I thought so! Here it is, in the list of the contents of Jerome's safe deposit box at the bank. One diamond ring, one pair of diamond cuff links. They have to be the same ones. These weren't stolen at all. He was setting him up. He was going to frame Buck Riley for stealing, and he was just trying to be sure he could make it stick, without getting hurt himself, when he talked to that lawyer. Why, that slimy so-and-so!'

'Why? Why would he do that? I swear that man was as twisted as a pretzel.' He chuckled. 'I once heard a man described as so twisted they had to screw him into the ground when he died. Sure fits our man, doesn't it!

'Now, Buck said earlier that Edwards had been hassling him lately, and he didn't know why. Looks like he was trying to get rid of him. Maybe he thought he would quit if he got on him enough. Then, when that didn't work, he decided to frame him and get him arrested. But why? Was he afraid of Buck? Maybe Buck knew something that would be a danger to Jerome. Something Buck saw or heard, and hadn't yet put together. Or maybe he had someone else in mind for the job. But, if that was so, why not just fire Buck? He didn't seem to have any trouble getting rid of employees.

'I still think if Buck wanted to kill his employer, this isn't the way he would do it. And I don't really think he's smart enough to figure out something like this. Anyway, why would he take him to the post office, of all places, when he could have done it anywhere. A road accident, something like that, would probably have worked. So, even though Buck had good reason to kill the man, this way doesn't make any sense. And besides, Buck wouldn't have had any way to get into the post office.

'That seems to be the stickler all along the way. Perolli, when are we going to get a break in this case? It seems that we turn one corner after another, but we haven't seen the light yet. I guess we have to start over,' he said, shuffling some of the papers on his desk and stacking them crookedly on the corner.

The Friendly Beasts

December 29, P.M.

Mr. Emerson, the recently elected District Attorney, walked into the police station in the middle of the afternoon, and was directed to Captain Charles's office.

'Captain Charles,' he said, entering, 'Daniel Emerson. I hear that your investigation of the murder of Jerome Edwards has been reaching our bailiwick.' He smiled and offered his hand.

Charles stood to greet him.

'Glad to see you, sir. Sit, won't you? Yeah, we had some questions to ask over there. I suspect you have talked to Cynthia, or she has talked to you. Is that right?'

Both men sat and took each other's measure. Charles was favorably impressed by the other man's demeanor and felt that Cynthia would have been treated fairly. He didn't know the man personally, but had heard nothing but good about him from other law-enforcement agencies. A tall, silver-haired man, with old-fashioned manners, he had been in politics in local government for many years and had earned the respect of the legal community. His election to the office of District Attorney had been a landslide. Very few votes had been cast for Jerome.

He replied now to Charles, 'Yes, Cynthia and I have spoken, tears were shed, and the air cleared. She really is a good girl, honest and capable. Jerome put her in a very uncomfortable position. I think she will learn from this and be stronger if something like this should ever happen again. And I think, and hope, that she knows she can confide in me in any like circumstance.'

'The reason I came to see you, Captain, is to set your mind at rest about Jerome Edwards's prying into Court House records. We know now what he had Cynthia copy, and we have looked into the matter thoroughly. We'd be happy to give you copies of all the findings. Seems Edwards was trying to find a scapegoat for the bridge collapse over in Port Haven, three years ago. He wanted to prove someone had taken bribes to use inferior materials, among other things. But we know the cause of the accident and no one can be blamed for it. Everyone involved had been cleared completely. So, even though Edwards got Cynthia in a mess, he didn't come up with any kind of proof for his suspicions. And I hardly think this could have had anything to do with his murder.'

'That's good to know. And it's one more end tied up. There seem to be too many loose ends in this affair,' Charles said.

The two men discussed the case, which would be Emerson's to prosecute when and if the killer could be found. Charles filled him in on what they had discovered so far, and some of the thoughts they had come up with. Emerson shook his head sadly.

'Such a waste of a good brain. Edwards had to have been quite intelligent to go as far as he did. What is that phrase? "If only he had used his talents for good instead of evil". Where does that come from? *Batman*, maybe?' he joked. 'Anyway, it certainly applies to this case.'

'Yeah, I would say he was a twisted son of a gun,' Charles nodded his head in agreement. Then he said, 'I'm glad you came by for another reason. We've come across something that should really interest you.'

He sent for the photos they had made from the film found in Edwards's bedroom and handed them to Emerson. As he leafed through them, Emerson was surprised and pleased to find evidence handed to him that might put away some of the gambling crowd that his office had been trying to indict for some time.

'This is amazing!' he said. 'Where did these come from?'

'We found the film hidden in a shoe in Jerome Edwards's bedroom closet when we searched yesterday. The lab had them developed and blown up for us. We didn't have any idea it could be something like this. We were told Jerome had been seen talking to some known gamblers in Rock Falls just shortly before he was killed, but this still came as a shock.'

'I can imagine,' the District Attorney said. 'You realized, of course, that these in themselves won't be enough to charge these men. We could certainly use the testimony of the person who took the pictures.'

'Yeah, true. But I don't think there's much hope for that. Whoever took these surely knows that Edwards has been murdered, which may have nothing to do with the photos, but it would sure make the photographer think twice about getting involved.'

Emerson said, 'You're right, unfortunately. But it's something positive to go with. Maybe some of our sources will have a name for us.'

'Well,' he said, standing, 'This has been most enlightening, and I'm sure the murder investigation is in good hands. We'll talk again soon, Captain.'

Charles stood also and said, 'It's a pleasure to meet you, sir, thanks for coming by. I hope we can have something solid for you very soon. And I'm relieved to know that Cynthia is all right. I really felt sorry for her. I know she had been put in a tight spot by Edwards.'

'All's well there now, Captain. Goodbye for now.'

The Captain spent the next hour reading and re-reading reports concerning the murder and working on other details that needed his attention.

Chambers came back, with little to add to the story of the fight between Jerome and Mark. It would seem the bartender only became aware of the argument when it reached the shouting level, and he claimed that since both men were shouting at the same time, he couldn't tell what the trouble was.

Soon after, while Chambers was still in the Captain's office discussing the matter with Charles, another patrolman entered with a thick stack of paper, copies of all the editorials which had been printed in the last year in the newspaper.

'Good. Thanks,' Charles said. 'Paul has been very thorough. These will be all the editorials Edwards wrote that may have a bearing on his killing. Quite a stack to wade through.'

Chambers groaned when he saw them.

'I suppose you're going to want me to read all these.'

Charles smiled. 'Yeah, it may be another wild goose chase, but maybe something will click. Start on it as soon as you can, and I'll give you a hand with it in the morning.'

I'll Be Home...

December 29, P.M.

As he sprawled in his favorite easy chair, a rerun of *The Waltons* was playing on TV, but Charles was not aware of it. Martha looked up from her knitting and said, 'This murder case is really getting you down, isn't it, dear.'

'Yeah, it's all so confusing. There's nothing to really get our teeth into. With a lot of crimes, we have too few suspects. This time we have too many!'

'Why don't you talk to me about it, and maybe something will come to you. It has worked before,' Martha said lightly.

'Okay,' Charles said, sitting a little straighter. 'There's his wife, and his daughter and his son-in-law, though I don't think any of the women would have had the strength to stab him that way. Then there's Stanford Bissell and Mark Kovich. They both certainly had reason to kill him. And Mark lied about not talking to Jerome in years, and he bought a gun just after a big noisy argument with Edwards, which sure sounds like he must have had murder in his heart. Or maybe he got it for protection because he had reason to fear Jerome. Sure would like to know what that argument was all about. Then these investigations Jerome had been conducting recently: the hospital fire (though I think I know what that was about), the fireworks factory accident and the bridge collapse. That's been explained, too. But what was he after? And did he pose a threat to someone because of these? And now we hear he has been involved with gamblers and trying to get something on the District Attorney and someone else in the Court House. Now does any of that make sense? Galloping galoshes! How could one man stir up so much trouble?'

Charles paused a moment, then continued, 'Okay. We found that Jerome was stabbed in that little room in the post office. That was a surprising thing, wasn't it! Did you ever notice that door?'

'No, I don't believe I did. And isn't it unusual for none of the people who work in the post office to be at least a little curious about it?'

'That's what I thought. But nobody even admits to knowing it was even there, which makes me think of Bissell and Duane. Both could have known about it, regardless of what they claim, they both hated Jerome, and it wouldn't have been too hard for them to get hold of a key to the room, and to the post office.

'Well, someone had to have a key to that room. There were no signs of a struggle and no signs that either of the doors were broken into. So it would follow that it was someone he knew, someone he must have trusted, at least not been afraid of. That doesn't sound like any of those from the gambling syndicate. Or somebody hired by them. He surely would have been a bit leery of meeting one of them in such an out-of-the-way place. But it surely is a possibility, after seeing those photographs we found in Jerome's closet.

'And you know, there's something funny about those things Jerome was poking into. Why now? He's been writing nasty editorials for a long time, but I don't remember him ever doing so much digging. Paul says Jerome's been doing all the legwork himself, not having someone else dig up stuff for him. He seems to have kept this all very secret. Why? And we haven't found any proof that he had found out anything. No papers or anything in his house or at the newspaper office. And that's strange, too. He had to have had some paperwork, some evidence of what he had hoped to uncover. He could have all that in his briefcase, I guess, but that hasn't turned up yet.

'Could it be he expected to gain something or other, not just dirt to print in his paper? There's something that's been nagging at me, but I just can't put my finger on it. Something I saw or heard that should have rung a bell.'

Charles stood and began pacing back and forth, digging his hands in his pockets. Martha looked up and said, 'Now don't get yourself all worked up. Sit down and get your mind on something else for a while. If you don't push it, maybe this little thing will come to you.'

'I can't think of anything else. This dratted thing has me

buffaloed.'

After a moment he sat again and continued, 'You know, if he was investigating all these things that Paul knew about, think how many other things he could have been looking into, that nobody knew about. In that case, all we've done so far could just be wasted time!

'All we really know for sure is that Edwards is dead, and up until now, I haven't run across anyone who shed any tears over his death. Pretty sad obituary, huh? I can just see the headline in *The Reporter*: "Jerome Edwards Dies – Who Cares?" then just a lot of white space. Actually though, that was quite a write-up in yesterday's paper. Wonder who wrote that? Paul, maybe? After all, Jerome *was* the owner of the paper and a pretty big wheel in the county and the state, so I guess he rated a big front-page story. It didn't say how he had cheated and defrauded and betrayed people, many of them the people closest to him, but I guess you can't put that sort of thing in the newspaper. The gossip mill and the local grapevine has been buzzing, though, with stories of his crooked deals.

'Paul told us he might have a buyer for the paper. If that happens, I wonder how it will change the newspaper, and if everyone will be kept on. There may be a big change in the slant the items in the news will take – more conservative or more liberal? Hard to tell. Then, of course, Mrs. Edwards will own all that now, which may make a difference. I told you about that, didn't I?'

'Yes, dear. I'm glad for her. Hers has not been a very happy life. Surely you couldn't really think of her as the killer, could you?'

'I just don't know. Some of the most unlikely people have turned out to be murderers.'

Charles stared unseeing at the TV screen. After some time he said, haltingly, 'Martha, I think I might have a small, very small, idea. I'm going to have to give this a lot more thought.'

Martha smiled and resumed counting stitches.

'Twas the Night Before

December 30, A.M.

After a troubled night, Charles arrived at the police station, yawning and rubbing his face. On the way to his office he ordered, 'Coffee! Lots of it!'

For the next hour and a half, Captain Charles sat at his desk, sometimes leafing through reports and making notes, sometimes staring into space. Finally, he went to the door and called to his sergeant. When Perolli entered he said, 'You know, old friend, I think I'm beginning to get a handle on this, getting some pieces put together. It's been six days since Edwards's murder, and we've covered a lot of ground, and I think I may finally be able to put all these pieces together. Now I want you to hold the fort for me. I've got to go a few places and find out a few things. So hang in here for me, will you? I'll be back when I'm back. Then I'll lay this all out for you.'

Perolli nodded and tapped Charles's shoulder as he passed him on the way to the door. Looking back as Perolli seated himself behind the desk, Charles said sadly, 'If I'm right...' then he shook his head and left.

During the rest of the day, Charles was seen in several places around town: some real estate offices, the planning office, the fire station, the lawyer's office, the bank. He was a veritable whirlwind of activity, and his notebook became filled with scribbled, virtually indecipherable jottings. Finally, at the end of the day, he wearily plodded back to the station and dropped into the visitor's chair in his office.

'I may be wrong, Perolli,' he said tiredly, 'but I think I have the answer. I want all the people we've talked to lately gathered together. Ask Aunt Ethel if we can meet at her house tomorrow evening.' He ticked them off on his fingers. 'Mark Kovich, Harold Duane, Stanford Bissell, Marjorie, Eric, the Judge, Lydia,

Cynthia and Paul.'

'See to it, will you, Perolli? I'm going to go home and get some sleep.'

Go Tell it on the Hilltop

December 31, P.M.

The Elms was lit warmly as Charles and Perolli drove up the winding road. Another police car followed. Charles reflected that it looked welcoming, but he doubted they would really be welcome, at least by one of the people inside.

The housekeeper opened the door at their knock and showed them into the room where all were gathered. This was the same room in which some of them had celebrated Christmas Day together. The fire blazed in the fireplace and the lamps gleamed on polished furniture. The tree was gone and where Christmas decorations had been, vases of flowers sat, along with knick-knacks and framed photographs. The room was warm, but the temperature might be said to be tense. Charles could almost feel the fear and uncertainty as he stepped into the room, Perolli close behind him. The other two policemen remained in the hall, just outside the door.

'Thank you all for coming,' Charles said, stepping toward the fire and warming his hands. Ethel stood to greet him.

'And thank you, Mrs. Wagner, for allowing us to come here in this way,' Charles added.

'It's quite all right, Captain. I hope you have news for us?'

Charles smiled at her and ten pairs of eyes stared warily at him.

'I'm sure you all know each other, except maybe for this young lady,' Charles began, waving in Cynthia's direction. 'This is Cynthia Gibbs, Mr. Emerson's secretary. She has been involved in this, as well as all of you, so we asked her to join us.'

Charles stood with his back to the fire, and Ethel moved back to the small sofa at right angles to the fireplace, sitting next to her daughter-in-law, Rose. David sat in a straight chair next to the sofa and captured his mother's hand in his as she sat. He and Rose had returned to Sunbury that afternoon, to spend New Year's Eve with Ethel and perhaps learn more about the murder that was disrupting all their lives.

Eric and Lydia sat close together on the other small sofa at the left of the fireplace and Marjorie sat stiffly erect in a chair at their side. Across the room, in matching wing chairs, Mark Kovich and Stanford Bissell moved restlessly. Judge Laurence was seated opposite them, next to a very nervous Cynthia Gibbs. Harold Duane perched on the edge of a chair a little way behind them, and Paul Brady stood near the door leading into the room.

'Why have you insisted that we come here, Captain?' sniffed Marjorie Edwards, scornfully. 'Are you trying to emulate Agatha Christie?'

'Now, Mother,' Lydia murmured.

Charles grinned and said, 'Yeah, something like that, I guess. If you all will be patient with me, I think I can clear up a lot of things and hopefully answer all your questions.'

Several of those listening shifted positions uneasily and glanced around the room. Ethel spoke from her seat near the fire. 'I'm sure we will all be very glad to have this settled. Please go on.'

'Thank you, Aunt Ethel. Well, let me begin by saying that we have investigated all of you and have found some surprising things. You are all involved in one way or another, and I thought this was the easiest way to let everyone know the truth. So please just let me do this my way, and we will get to the bottom of this case.

'First, Eric, we couldn't find anyone who was sure of seeing you in the stores as you said you were at the time of the murder. You certainly had cause to hate Mr. Edwards.' He held his hand up as Eric started out of his seat. 'But we were sure you couldn't have killed him, for several other reasons. The same motive applies to Lydia, but again we discarded that.

'Now, Mark, you certainly had bad feelings toward Jerome. And you had made threats against him, hadn't you?'

Mark glared at the policeman and said, 'I had good reason to hate him, since he pretty much ruined my life, but I didn't kill him.'

'You said you were in that bar that night, but Judge Laurence says he saw you near the post office.'

Mark jumped to his feet and shouted, 'That's a lie! I wasn't anywhere near there!'

'Well, I could have been mistaken,' the Judge said, 'but I was sure it was him I saw.'

'We didn't find anyone else in the bar who remembered seeing you there Christmas Eve either.'

'It was a madhouse that night! I sat in the back and drank, and you can't prove otherwise!'

'All right, calm down, Mark.' Charles watched as Mark resumed his seat, still fuming. Then he said, 'We have other questions to ask you. For example, you told us you hadn't talked to Jerome in years, yet witnesses tell us that you had a loud, violent argument with him just a week before he was killed. And right after that you went out and bought a gun. Care to tell us about that?'

Mark squirmed in his seat, his face turning red.

'I *did* want to kill him. But I came to my senses before I could do anything.'

'That why you bought the gun?'

'Yes. He claimed I owed him money, from way back when I owned the newspaper, and he said if I didn't come through with a very large sum, he would see I lost my job at Preston's. I got so damned mad, I could have killed him right there in the bar. If I'd had a gun then, I probably would have.' Mark scowled at Charles and at the room in general. 'But he wasn't shot, was he?' he said.

'Right. He wasn't,' Charles replied. He turned from Mark and addressed the group. 'Now, this happened at the post office. So, Harold, you were on our list. Who better to have the means to open the door into the building, and that door inside the building? All we have is your word that you didn't know about that room. But your alibi checked out and we had to cross you off our list.'

'Well, thank you for that, Charles,' Duane said sarcastically. 'All I told you was the truth. If you'd just believed me, we wouldn't have had to go through all this.'

Charles shook his head, and said, 'We also looked into the backgrounds of all the postal employees and couldn't find anyone who had any kind of contact with Jerome.'

'I told you that,' Duane smirked.

'But we had to check. Now, Mrs. Edwards,' Charles continued, turning toward her. 'You claimed you were with your daughter at home for that period of time. But when our men finally found you that evening, you were just turning into your driveway. Mind telling us where you really were?'

Marjorie reddened and said, 'It has nothing to do with all of this. If you must know, I was with my friend Jim Patterson, helping him decorate his apartment.'

'Mother! You never told us!' Lydia exclaimed.

Charles smiled at Marjorie's discomfort, and turned his attention to Stanford Bissell. 'Well, then, we come to Mr. Bissell. We found that he had been paying blackmail to Edwards.'

Bissell looked pleadingly at Charles, who continued, 'The reason for the blackmail is a personal matter and not important to the whole issue.'

Stanford slumped back in his chair. 'We did think for a while it could be you, Stanford, especially with your connection to the post office.'

Addressing the group in general, Charles went on, 'Which brings us to the mystery of that locked door in the post office. Who knew about it? Well, Duane and Stanford must have, though they both say they had no knowledge of it. Then something else came up when I was looking over the architect's plans for the building. Your brother-in-law was the contractor for the building, wasn't he, Judge?'

'Why, yes, Captain, I believe he was,' answered the judge. 'But that was a very long time ago.'

'Yes, longer ago than the fire at the fireworks factory.'

Judge Laurence turned pale as he asked, 'What does that have to do with this event?'

Ignoring the judge for a moment, Charles continued, 'So many things happened at the same time. The break-in at the newspaper office, for instance. The burglary tied Jerome to gambling interests. We may never know what was taken from the safe. We are certain, however, that a well known felon, Willie Best, is the person who burglarized the safe. His fingerprints were found at the scene, and Willie has disappeared. Nothing more has come to light in this matter, though we're pretty sure he was hired by some very rough characters. The same ones Jerome was seen talking to in Rock Falls two days before his death. So, if the witnesses were right in thinking Jerome was being threatened that day, and it looks like he was, then Jerome must have had something in the safe that would be a danger to these people. We can only guess what it might be, but we have a good idea of what it was, and that will all come out in the near future.

'But what the break-in did do was to make us think about what we could have expected to find in the safe. Maybe the burglar took it all with him. Maybe it was never there. But it made us look a little closer at the things Jerome had been investigating, according to Paul.'

Charles nodded in Paul's direction.

'So we started backtracking on Jerome's trail. Cynthia had told us he was looking for records from the Court House, and for a while we thought it might have something to do with the collapse of that bridge over in Port Haven. He was curious about contractor's bids. Maybe he suspected cost cutting, shoddy workmanship, graft, something of that sort. Nothing was suspected at the time, and it was very thoroughly investigated. We've gone over that again, and we find there was no wrongdoing there. I don't know what Jerome had found or suspected in that incident, but he was wrong. Mr. Emerson has assured us that this was a dead end.

'But Jerome was also looking into the fireworks accident that killed his uncle. That seemed very odd, since it had happened so many years ago. So, following every lead, no matter how obscure, we followed in Jerome's footsteps again, looking back in the old issues of the newspaper. In there, the day before the fire, there was a report of a hit-and-run accident. A young boy was killed, and the driver of the car had not been found.'

Charles paused and faced Judge Laurence.

'You were driving that car, weren't you, Judge? And Al Wagner was with you. Al was going to go to the police and tell all, when you confronted him at the factory. But you couldn't let that happen, could you, Judge?'

Charles watched as the judge sank deeper in his chair. He put his hand over his eyes and said, in a very faint voice, 'The fire was an accident. I never meant it to happen. We fought. I knocked him down, and then the fire started. I ran. I should have gone back in, or gotten help to save him, but I was afraid. And the fire was raging. I'm sorry, Ethel.'

Ethel said, very quietly, 'I have always been sure there was more to the story. Al was much too careful to have fire anywhere in the building.'

'There was a picture of you, Judge, in the paper that day. You were smoking a pipe. Did you have your pipe lit when you were there with Al?' Charles asked.

Judge Laurence nodded wearily. 'I laid it down when we started to argue. It must have started some papers burning.'

'The picture in the paper was because of your appointment to the Circuit Court.'

'That's why I couldn't let Al confess to the police about the hit-and-run accident,' the judge said slowly. 'It would have ruined my chances. I could never have sat on the bench with a conviction like that on my record.'

'So Jerome figured all of this out. What did he want from you? Money?'

'No. He wanted – he insisted – that I use my influence to make sure the new highway went through property he had purchased.'

'I thought that might be why he was buying all those parcels of land. But why didn't you just go along with him?'

'If I had, there would have been something else he'd force me to do, and he could have told his story any time. I had to stop him.'

'What about the key to the post office?'

The Judge sighed, and with a bitter laugh, said, 'My brother-in-law was a bit of a Don Juan in those days. We were both young, he hadn't yet married my sister. He kept a set of keys after the building was completed, and we used to play "post office" in that room in the building. You remember the old game. We thought it was a huge joke. If any of the people who were with us there were still alive, they probably could have told you about that room. But they're all gone.'

After a pause, he said, 'We almost got caught once and never did it again. But I've had those keys all these years. It was easy to get Jerome to meet me there. He never thought an old codger like me could ever harm him. He thought he was invincible. He went into that room with me when I told him there was something hidden there that would be evidence against Duane. He was determined to get him out of his job as Postmaster. I was going to leave him there, but he didn't die right away. So I opened the other door and pushed him out. I don't know how he managed to make it all the way down the steps.'

A shocked silence greeted the judge's confession.

'We found these gloves in your car, sir,' Charles said, pulling a plastic bag from an inside pocket of his coat. 'They are covered with blood. I'm surprised you didn't get rid of them.'

'I have been in a kind of daze, I think. I didn't remember leaving the gloves there.'

'Did you have his briefcase, too? We haven't been able to find it.'

'I took it with me because I was sure he would have some proof of his claims against me. I burned all the papers that were in it and I cut up the briefcase and buried it in the garbage.'

'One more thing, Judge. I'm curious. How did you just happen to have a knife handy when you met with Jerome?'

Judge Laurence, with his hand shading his eyes, replied shakily. 'I took it with me because I didn't trust Jerome. I think I had some idea of threatening him with it. Or maybe I took it for protection. I don't know...' his voice trailed off.

'And what happened to the knife?' Charles asked.

'It's buried in the garbage along with the briefcase.'

'All right. I'm afraid I'm going to have to ask you to come with us now, Judge,' Charles said, motioning to the two policemen standing in the doorway. They came forward and led the judge from the room. He left without looking at any of the others gathered there.

There was a general sighing and release from tension in the group. For a while no one spoke. Then Ethel said, 'I've always had a funny feeling about Tom, and I couldn't understand why. I guess he did all he could to help me out of a feeling of remorse and guilt. But I can't believe he really meant to kill Al. They had always been such close friends.'

'I'm positive it was an accident, as the experts said at the time,' Charles replied. 'But it wouldn't have happened except for the fight between Al and the judge. I'm sorry we had to bring all this back to you, but it had to be brought out in the open.'

Charles picked up his coat and hat and prepared to leave.

'Well, we'll be moving along now,' he said. 'Thank you, Aunt Ethel, for allowing us to meet here.'

Charles shook hands with Ethel and those sitting near him as he headed out the door, nodding at Paul who still stood in the doorway.

Perolli hesitated, then all in the room sat open-mouthed in amazement as he spoke the only words they had heard him utter.

'Happy New Year to all,' he said.